THE IMPOSSIBLE PREFECT

"Look, over there! A fellow getting on to the lobby roof!"

(*See* p. 111.)

THE
IMPOSSIBLE PREFECT

by
HUBERT ROBINSON

Illustrated by Savile Lumley

THOMAS NELSON AND SONS LTD
LONDON EDINBURGH PARIS MELBOURNE
TORONTO AND NEW YORK

THOMAS NELSON AND SONS LTD
Parkside Works Edinburgh 9
3 Henrietta Street London WC2
312 Flinders Street Melbourne C1
5 Parker's Buildings Burg Street Cape Town

THOMAS NELSON AND SONS (CANADA) LTD
91–93 Wellington Street West Toronto 1

THOMAS NELSON AND SONS
385 Madison Avenue New York 17

SOCIÉTÉ FRANÇAISE D'EDITIONS NELSON
25 rue Henri Barbusse Paris V°

CONTENTS

LIST OF ILLUSTRATIONS

ix

THE IMPOSSIBLE PREFECT

CHAPTER I

THE HEAD SPRINGS A SURPRISE

THE Rev. Pelham Alcott, headmaster of Melhurst, leaned forward in his study chair and pressed the bell on the desk before him.

"Have Mr. Darrell of Reed's House sent to me, will you, Baxter?" he said to his butler a few moments later. "I saw him arrive about half an hour ago."

The butler bowed and withdrew.

As the door closed the Head rose and approached the open window. As he gazed down at the quadrangle he frowned and tapped the sill with his fingers.

Below him was a scene of confusion. All over

the quadrangle were boxes and portmanteaux, for this was the opening day of the summer term. Some boys were standing about, exchanging news of the holidays ; others were hurrying to and fro, whilst new arrivals were constantly entering through the gateways. Amid the throng the porters laboured, carrying luggage into the buildings.

But the Head saw little of this ; he turned away and began pacing up and down the room, as though preoccupied with a problem. Then he came back to the window, his fingers tapping restlessly as before.

Suddenly there was a knock at the door, and in response to his " Come in," a tall dark boy of about eighteen entered the room.

" Ah, here you are, Darrell," said the Head genially. " Sit down, will you." He motioned him to a chair. " Had good holidays ? "

" Yes, thank you, sir."

The Head sat down in his own chair on the other side of the desk and gazed intently at the new-comer.

" I have sent for you, Darrell," he said in a

different tone, " because I have something important to say to you. First of all, may I ask what your parents thought of your last report? "

Darrell flushed, cleared his throat, and shifted uneasily on his chair.

" Not much, sir," he said at length.

" That, I presume, is putting it mildly," went on the Head. " Your report was one of the worst in the form. Your form master described your general conduct as outrageous. Other masters were hardly flattering concerning your work for the term. And this bad report, Darrell, is only one of many, dating back almost to the time when you first came to Melhurst.

" A close study of your record has revealed an interesting fact. Although your work is undoubtedly poor, it has invariably improved during the winter term, enabling you to scrape through into a higher form with your friends. This is proof that you are not a dunce, Darrell; you are capable of good work but refuse to apply yourself to it. Moreover, your behaviour out of school hours has been far from satisfactory. You seem to delight in breaking rules and disregarding authority. You and two others, Larkin and Collinson, have caused a good deal of trouble in the past. I don't know what your parents have said to you on the subject, but I tell you frankly, Darrell, this conduct has got to stop. And I am determined to stop it."

The Head paused for a moment, watching the boy's downcast face. The faint murmur of many voices drifted up from the quadrangle.

"What I have now decided to do," he resumed, "may considerably surprise you. Although you are only in the Fifth Form, in my opinion you are mentally equipped for the Sixth. For that reason I am moving you up into the Sixth without delay. This will do much to separate you from your two confederates. Also, in the Sixth you will come a great deal under my own jurisdiction, and I shall see to it that you work hard.

"But that is not all. The fact remains that you dislike authority. Therefore I am going to make you a prefect in the place of Aguilar who left last term. This office carries with it a great deal of responsibility, which will, I hope, be the means of curbing that childish tendency in your nature."

Again there was a silence. Darrell contemplated the Head with mouth agape and eyes staring.

" Move me up into the Sixth and make me a prefect ? " he said incredulously.

The Head nodded.

" But, sir, you can't mean it. Surely you're only joking. Why——" Darrell broke into a laugh, which was instantly silenced as his eyes met those of the Head.

" What, Darrell, are your objections ? " inquired the Head smoothly.

" Why, sir, I'm not due for a remove into the Sixth for another two terms. And as for making me a prefect, the fellows would simply laugh at me. I shouldn't have any authority over them at all."

" You could have if you chose to exercise it."

" But how can I, sir, after—well, after I've been all that you said I have ? "

" That is one of the reasons, Darrell, why I am adopting this course. I want to discover whether or not you have the character to end your old way of living, and begin another which will be a credit to yourself and the school. Regard it as a test—a test that will prove your true worth to Melhurst. If you fail—if, in other words, you go on as you have been doing —I shall be greatly disappointed. But I hope that will not be the case. I want to see you come out of this test with flying colours, and settle down to become a sober and hard-working member of the school."

" Couldn't I do that without becoming a prefect ? " asked Darrell hopefully.

The Head laughed.

" Do you know, Darrell," he said, " that you are the first boy I have met in my career as a schoolmaster, who has objected to being made a prefect ? "

" I never was keen on that kind of thing, sir," confessed Darrell.

" No doubt," commented the Head dryly. "I gathered as much a long while ago. And now the blow has fallen. You are a prefect at last."

Darrell knew that gentle, chiding sarcasm of

the Head's. It made you look a fool and feel that you were receiving sympathy because of it.

"Supposing, sir," said Darrell, "that you didn't find me big enough for this test—if I didn't make a good prefect at all, would you consider giving the position to some one else instead ? "

"Let us put it another way," said the Head. "You mean that if you made a thorough nuisance of yourself, would I feel bound to give up the idea and let matters continue as before ? "

Darrell flushed, but made no reply.

"Listen, Darrell," said the Head, leaning forward. "You are captain of cricket this term. If I felt there was cause enough I should depose you from the captaincy rather than from the prefecture. And, unless I am mistaken, that would be the last thing you desire."

The Head was not mistaken. Ever since Darrell had come to Melhurst, as a small boy of thirteen, it had been his dream to become captain of cricket. Possessed of a natural aptitude for games, at cricket he excelled, and on cricket he concentrated. In the summer months he went in for intensive practice during term and holidays as well.

Before long he was a marked man ; by the time he was sixteen, and in the Fourth, he was already a prominent member of the first cricket eleven. This term, in the place of Sims, who left at the end of the previous season, Darrell was to take over the captaincy of cricket.

And Darrell knew the Head knew that he would submit to anything rather than allow this cherished dream to be dispelled when it was about to become reality.

Nevertheless, he made a last despairing effort.

" There's another aspect of the matter to be considered, sir," he said. " The other prefects would refuse to have me as one of them. Why, I'm the very last person in the world to take over Aguilar's position. It will result "—a brilliant idea, this—" in authority at Melhurst becoming a mere byword."

" Ingenious, Darrell," commented the Head. " But it will hardly be as bad as that. If you show yourself to be firm enough, authority at Melhurst will benefit rather than suffer."

He opened a drawer and began rummaging in the contents.

"And now let me give you your prefect's badge. You will take over Aguilar's study, No. 12 on the prefects' corridor."

Giving Darrell the badge, the Head shook hands heartily.

"I expect you are thinking hard things of me for beginning your term in such a fashion, Darrell, but in time to come you'll realize that it was all for the best. Do your utmost and you'll pull through."

Darrell gave an inward groan, but nodded in agreement.

"I suppose so, sir." He walked slowly to the door. "And thank you, sir," he added. Though what he was thanking the Head for he could not have explained.

Descending the stairs, he mingled with the crowd outside in the quadrangle. Desperately he wondered whether he was dreaming, and whether he would wake up and find that he was still a member of the Fifth, instead of . . .

Darrell groaned in dismay.

There were four houses at Melhurst—Reed's, Segal's, Lancaster's, and Everton's—each house having only three prefects. Consequently, there was always keen interest among the five hundred boys as to the filling of these positions when they became vacant. Usually the Head appointed boys highest in school order, but an occasional exception was made in favour of individuals particularly brilliant at games.

But Darrell did not want to be a prefect. His dislike of restraint of any kind, combined with a gift of repartee and a talent for practical joking, had, he considered, removed him from any danger of enlistment on the side of authority.

As a magnet attracts steel, so Darrell had attracted Larkin and Collinson. The trio was soon marked down by masters, and either admired or dreaded by boys. A couple of terms ago they had painted red stripes on the white front of the "Peal o' Bells," the public house in the small village of Coombe. Rumour connected this midnight escapade with Darrell, Larkin, and Collinson, but owing to lack of definite evidence they were allowed to go unpunished.

Again, the three of them were responsible when the school bell boomed in the small hours and woke every one up. This time they were discovered, with the result that none of them could sit down properly for a week.

Also, they were the authors of a school magazine which had to cease publication after the issue of its first number, owing to the highly libellous nature of its contents.

Now a calamity had happened to the gang, and Darrell had to break the news to the two others.

He looked about him in the quadrangle, but could not see them. Deciding, however, to try the tuckshop, he was rewarded by the sight of Larkin and Collinson refreshing themselves after their journey.

Larkin was long and thin, Collinson short and plump.

" Hallo, you fathead," said the latter. " Been here long ? "

" About an hour, and it's been the longest hour in my life."

"What's up ? " inquired Larkin. "Anything happened ? "

"No, nothing much," replied Darrell wearily. "The world turned upside down, that's all."

"Bad as that ? " said Larkin sympathetically. "You ought to take liver salts."

"It isn't my liver," groaned Darrell. "One could put up with that. But this . . ."

"Tell us about it," suggested Collinson.

With his elbows on the table in front of him, and his head leaning on his hands, Darrell explained what had passed between himself and the Head.

When he had finished, there was a silence among the three which lasted for fully a minute. They sat staring at one another, Larkin and Collinson as if they had been hit heavily over the head, and Darrell with a kind of moody satisfaction at having startled them so effectively.

"Well ! " began Larkin, but further words eluded him.

"But the whole thing's preposterous," almost shouted Collinson. "He can't do it. He'll have the whole school against him. As soon

as it becomes known there'll be such an outcry
that he'll have to alter his decision. Why, everybody thought that Kenton would be the next
prefect as a matter of course. The Head can't
go playing ducks and drakes with the prefect
system. The fellows won't stand for it."

" He won't mind that," said Darrell. " Bless
you, our Head thrives on opposition of all
kinds. It's the very meat of his existence."

" He ought to be shot at dawn," exploded
Larkin.

" Why wait till dawn ? " enquired Collinson
savagely.

" What are you going to do about it ? "
asked Larkin.

Darrell shrugged his shoulders.

" What can I do about it ? "

" Run amuck. Start breaking one school
rule after another. Use your authority to mess
things up in general. He won't have a prefect
for long who plays about like Charlie Chaplin.
He'll have to depose you."

" He's thought of that," said Darrell. " He
told me that any unruly behaviour would mean

my losing the cricket captaincy before the prefecture. He must have spent hours beforehand closing up every loophole of escape. I tell you, he's so clever he ought to be twins."

" But there must be a way to get out of it. Supposing the fellows won't have you as a prefect, supposing the kids refuse to obey you, what then ? Although there mayn't be any active opposition, he'll come to realize that the thing's a farce and appoint Kenton instead. You could help, not by mucking about openly, but by going to work in a more insidious way. Be very lenient with the kids and they'll soon learn to make the most of their opportunities. You'll be a prefect in name only ; and, dash it all ! he can't say it's your fault if you're not a success."

" I shall still be a prefect officially," said Darrell. "I shall be overloaded with responsibilities of various kinds. I shall even have to take detention, I who was in detention myself last term."

" How about our trying to do something for you ? " said Collinson.

" In what way ? "

" Supposing we approached the Head and asked him, very nicely, to alter his decision. Blither a lot of bilge to him. Tell him that we actually left you crying, because you're afraid you won't be able to do the harder work set in the Sixth—all that sort of rot. We might be able to produce some effect."

Darrell shook his head.

" No go. You know what he's like."

" Then it's good-bye to the gang," said Larkin. " You'll be in another form and in another study, having to look like *Eric or Little by Little* the whole day long. We shall simply have to disband and join the school choir."

" Disband ? " repeated Darrell, starting up. " Not if I know it. Here, fill up with ginger beer, and let's drink to the health of the gang. Long may it reign."

" Health to the gang," repeated Collinson and Larkin, rising and waving their glasses aloft. " Long may it reign."

And all three drank together.

then digressed a little, comparing Melhurst with other public schools to the detriment of the latter, mentioned one or two past achievements of Melhurst, and finished with a lecture on the need for a serious spirit in all school activities.

He spoke for nearly twenty minutes, and when he had done, the word "school" seemed to boom faintly in the air. There was a sigh of relief from the listeners, and much scraping of chairs, as though to intimate : " Well, now that's finished, perhaps we can get some tea."

" There's just one thing more before you go," said Goulding.

A perceptible groan rose from the assembly, but Goulding either did not hear or did not heed it.

" It concerns that chap Darrell," he went on.

Darrell was Goulding's *bête noire*. Darrell loathed Goulding for being, as he told Larkin, too good to be true. And the animosity between them was deepened by Darrell's seizing every chance of ragging the school captain.

On one celebrated occasion, when Goulding was taking detention, Darrell had risen from his

seat and said, in tones trembling with anger :
" Please, Goulding, some one's spilt ink all
over my book." And a view of his book
disclosed a large pool of ink almost covering
an open page. After asking, unavailingly, for
the culprit to stand forward, Goulding delivered
a short lecture on owning up to misdemeanours;
then, approaching with blotter in hand, he
attempted to mop up the ink, and found it to
be a solid imitation.

Goulding never forgave Darrell for fooling
him on that occasion; and even now, as he
addressed the prefects, the memory of the
episode brought a flush to his cheeks.

" Darrell," he said, " has long been the cause
of a great deal of indiscipline. He and those
two friends of his have played the silly ass for
years, making Reed's House a laughing-stock
in the eyes of the other houses. If Reed's
House knew it, they wouldn't put up with
Darrell at all. But they think he's clever, and
encourage him to go on making a fool of the
house as well as of himself.

" Now this term Darrell becomes captain of

cricket. This is one of the most important positions in the school, and it's unfortunate that Darrell should hold it. I don't deny that he's good at cricket, but it would be better if a prefect were given so great a responsibility. Frankly, I don't think that Darrell's the best man for the job. I'm afraid he'll use his new position to make himself a greater nuisance than ever.

" So I propose that we have him up before us now, and tell him that we're not going to stand any more nonsense from him. A prefect still stands higher in the school than the captain of cricket. A straight talk might do him good."

" You mean, tick him off," said Humphreys, a friend of Goulding's.

" That's the idea," said Goulding, and the rest of the prefects voiced their approval.

Undoubtedly speech-making was a poor way of beginning a term, but ticking somebody off, and the captain of cricket at that, was quite a different matter.

Kenton, being the youngest present, was dispatched in search of Darrell. Then Goulding, standing on the hearth-rug with his hands in his trousers pockets, and the others, sitting back importantly in their chairs, waited with pleasurable anticipation for Kenton's return.

After about ten minutes the door opened and Kenton came in, followed by Darrell.

" Here he is," he said.

" Shut the door, Darrell," Goulding directed.

Darrell stared round the room, concealing any surprise he might have felt. Then he set a heel against the door and slammed it behind him.

CHAPTER III

DARRELL IS TICKED OFF

" YOU might do it quietly while you're about it," said Goulding.

" Sorry," said Darrell.

Pulling a chair towards him, he sat down, uninvited, and gazed at the others with inquiring eyes. Goulding was a little taken aback, for he had meant to have Darrell standing before him.

However, Goulding himself half-stood, half-sat, with one leg over the corner of the table, and so looked down on Darrell as he began to speak.

" We want to have a talk with you, Darrell, about things in general."

" That's very nice of you," said Darrell.

" The fact is," Goulding went on, " we're rather troubled about your new position as captain of cricket. I think it's best to put things quite plainly, then we know how we stand. In the past you've made a nuisance of yourself. And you may think that as captain of cricket you can now be a bigger nuisance than ever."

He turned to the others.

" That's right, isn't it ? "

They murmured assent.

" And so we've summoned you before us to tell you that we're not going to have any rotting from you in the future. Unless you settle down you'll find yourself in hot water very quickly."

" Oceans of it," said Humphreys.

" Up till now," went on Goulding, " besides playing the fool, you've *made* a thorough fool of yourself. Only you don't appear to know it." He paused to let this point sink in. " You and Larkin and Collinson have been undermining law and order not only in Reed's House, but throughout the school. When you three kick over the traces, a fag in the First thinks he can do the same, and so the game goes on. You have done a good deal towards pulling Melhurst down from the position we hold among the public schools to-day.

" I don't know whether the Head realizes it, but I and my colleagues certainly do. So either you cease this idiotic behaviour or we shall take all measures in our power to stop you from becoming a menace to the traditions and ideals of Melhurst."

Goulding had now warmed to his theme, and was thoroughly enjoying himself.

" But," he resumed, " a lot depends on you. If you determine to turn over a new leaf, then I for one shall be very glad. Instead of working against the school you can pull your weight for its good, and so help to restore some of the prestige which, owing to you, it has lost in the past.

" We don't want to be too hard on you at the beginning of the term, but we all thought it fair to warn you, in the hope that you will alter your attitude to the masters and to ourselves in the future."

" I see," said Darrell. While Goulding was speaking he had sat back in his chair, his attention fixed mainly on the speaker, his face impassive as a block of wood.

" What exactly has been the matter with my attitude up till now ? " he asked.

" Well," said Goulding, " I should have thought you'd have known as well as any one. Your manner to me especially has been insolent. You have never seemed to realize that I'm school captain. Because you're captain of cricket you mustn't think that you can regard me and the prefects as—as——" Again he paused.

" As maggots," supplied Darrell helpfully.

" As maggots," repeated Goulding. " And —er, no, no, I don't mean that," he stammered. " I don't mean that at all. For heaven's sake stop playing the goat, Darrell. Can't you be serious for once ? "

" Sorry. I was only trying to be helpful."

" Well, I think that's about all," said Goulding, turning to the others. " Don't you ? "

Goulding was gratified that Darrell had attempted no back-chat, but the other prefects had looked for some opposition on Darrell's part, and were rather disappointed that he had made no defence.

However, they agreed, and said so.

" Yes, that's about all," was Kenton's contribution.

Darrell turned his attention to Kenton, and did not like him. He had a large, moist, red mouth that impressed Darrell unfavourably.

"What," he asked, "is Kenton doing here ? He's not a prefect."

" Not at this moment," said Goulding. " But he's bound to be nominated by the Head in the next couple of days. So we had him along here with us."

" But——" said Darrell, staring. " But——" and he burst into a howl of laughter.

" What on earth's the matter ? " asked Goulding. " Have you gone potty ? "

" Nothing ! " gasped Darrell. " Nothing at all—that is, I—no, no, nothing ! "

Humphreys looked across at Everton and tapped his forehead significantly.

" I hope you'll excuse me," blurted Darrell, getting up, with his handkerchief to his face. " Bu—but—— oh, ha, ha, ha ! "

He staggered to the door, and without troubling to shut it, left them.

" What on earth's the matter with him ? " asked Goulding.

" He always was a bit bughouse," said Humphreys.

At that moment a fag knocked and came in with a note for Goulding.

" Pleath, the Head told me to give you thith," he lisped. " There'th no anther."

He trotted out again.

Goulding opened the note and read it. He read it again, and a third time.

" What on earth ? " he ejaculated. His face was quite white.

" What is it ? " asked Humphreys, getting up and peering over his shoulder.

Then : " Oh, my sainted aunt ! " exclaimed Humphreys in his turn.

" What's the matter ? " asked Everton. " Anything serious ? "

" Listen," said Humphreys in a strained voice. " This is what it says " :

" ' DEAR GOULDING,—I am having Darrell moved up into the Sixth Form and made a prefect in Aguilar's place. I have already apprised Darrell of this change, and I hope that you will make him at home until I have time to explain things more fully to you.

PELHAM ALCOTT.' "

The prefects looked at one another, too astonished to speak. Darrell's laughter could still be heard faintly in the distance.

CHAPTER IV

DARRELL PROVES HIS WORTH

NO one besides the astounded prefects, except Larkin, Collinson, and Kenton, knew that day of Darrell's new appointment. Darrell, Larkin, and Collinson told no one about it because no one would have believed them. The prefects and Kenton were too thunderstruck to do more than grumble about it among themselves.

So it was that, next morning, when the Head strode into Hall where the school was assembled, only a few boys knew what to expect. The Head, having a sense of drama, always kept his most important announcements till the end of a speech. And when at length he reached the matter of Darrell's prefecture, a rustle of astonished movement was followed by absolute silence.

Calmly the Head gave reasons for his unusual action. Darrell, he told the school, he considered too old to remain in the Fifth, and as the captain of cricket was usually a prefect, he had thought it best to nominate Darrell to the vacant prefecture. There were also other reasons which confirmed his choice in this instance.

" The cunning blighter ! " whispered Larkin to Collinson. " He knows how to put a thing over ! "

And whilst the surprise of the prefects had been mingled with dismay, the rest of the school received the news with a pleasurable amazement. Here was something to break the monotony of settling down to work !

That afternoon the thing was discussed from the Sixth Form down to the First. Cricket practice was mainly an occasion for intensive gossip. Wicket-keepers crouched very near to batsmen, who swiped aimlessly at balls, while they conversed in eager tones ; bowlers exchanged opinions with umpires in serial form when they ran to the wicket to bowl ; and fielders rested their hands on the ground, palms upward, as fielders do, and bent their heads aside to speak to one another.

Darrell, Larkin, and Collinson were nowhere to be seen, having gone for a walk to give the excitement an opportunity to subside.

After cricket practice a rumour spread to the effect that the prefects, headed by Goulding, were going in a body to the Head to lodge a protest. Instantly there was a rush in the direction of the Head's house, round the entrance of which a crowd quickly collected. And through this crowd came the prefects, looking very grim and determined, like ten Daniels going to beard a lion.

They were not kept waiting for long. The Head received them in his study and pleasantly inquired the nature of their business.

The spokesman, of course, was Goulding. Goulding stated the prefects' case in his most reasonable manner. He and the other prefects did not want Darrell as one of them—Darrell, the most disorderly boy in the school, who would bring into ridicule the office of prefect

41

and all those who were his colleagues. Kenton was the best man for the position. Kenton, now, Kenton . . . and so on. Goulding said a great deal, whilst the Head gazed silently at the desk before him.

At last Goulding finished, and he and the others waited for the Head's reply. For what seemed a long time the Head sat without speaking, but with the hint of a smile at the corners of his mouth. The prefects became uneasy. Some of them even coughed and moved a little in the direction of the door, as though to say : " Well, perhaps we'd better leave it at that. But they were thinking : " What fools we were to have been let in for this by Goulding. We might have known. . . ."

At last the Head began to speak. At first he was only heard by those within the study, but soon his voice reached those outside. The crowd beneath his window listened in an appalled silence.

" There never was," they said to themselves, " a row like this."

Nothing so roused the Head's wrath as the

questioning of his decisions once they had been publicly pronounced. His word, he considered, should be final. Impertinence, lying, stealing, laziness—he had dealt with all sorts of failings and misdeeds in his time, and had sometimes been surprisingly lenient with the most flagrant of sinners. But when a boy openly opposed him the Head became a changed man. He had made Darrell a prefect, and therefore it should be taken as final that Darrell was to remain a prefect. From Darrell himself he had expected some show of opposition, but from the other prefects he required nothing but obedience in the matter.

By the time he had finished, the prefects were effectually informed in this respect. Let him, they thought, make prefects of First Form fags if he liked. Their mental and physical condition was very different from that of half an hour before. Then they had been fine examples of British youth ; now they were as reeds broken by a storm. When they were allowed to depart, the crowd in the quadrangle opened almost silently to let them pass. Here and there somebody whistled. No words were needed.

The new appointment being established, the school began to wonder how Darrell would take his sudden ascent to a position of authority. Would he behave as a prefect should, or would he continue to behave as before ?

An answer to this problem was provided that night by Darrell himself.

At Melhurst each prefect had charge of a dormitory, and it was his duty to look in occasionally before he went to bed himself, to ensure that the inhabitants were conducting themselves in an orderly manner. Thus Darrell, although he detested having to act as if he were a master on the prowl, went to assure himself that everything was as it should be. He decided to bob in and out as quickly as possible—with the result that when he entered no one knew that he was there.

The dormitory presented an interesting scene. Tallboys and Vidler, the two biggest fellows in the room, were trying to overturn Sharpe, the smallest fellow in the room, into a blanket spread out on a bed. The remainder of those present lay or sat watching the struggle. To Darrell the situation was plain. Tallboys and Vidler were wanting to toss Sharpe in the blanket.

We are informed nowadays that school bullying has died out. This is untrue. Whilst it does not flourish as in the days of Tom Brown, when various unfortunates were roasted before the fire like meat, it is still carried on wherever there are bullies.

Tallboys and Vidler were bullies. They never hurt their victims badly, but they enjoyed upsetting smaller boys into puddles, pushing them from one to the other like sacks of potatoes, and rolling them over on the ground and sitting on them. In the absence of the prefect in charge they held sway in the dormitory.

Just as they had succeeded in toppling Sharpe on to the bed, Darrell advanced down the room.

" I say," he said loudly.

Tallboys and Vidler released Sharpe as if by magic. Sharpe got off the bed, evidently much relieved by Darrell's presence. And the three looked at Darrell and waited.

The others were surprised and delighted. Here, they felt, was a Situation. They, too, watched and waited.

"What," asked Darrell of Tallboys and Vidler, "has Sharpe done to deserve this?"

They shifted uneasily.

"He was being cheeky," said Tallboys.

"Is that true?" asked Darrell of Sharpe.

"Well," said Sharpe, "I called Vidler a silly fathead, but there's nothing much in that. Fellows are always calling one another silly fatheads. And, anyway, he is a silly fathead."

"Your logic is faultless," Darrell told him, and turned to the other two. "Am I to take it that Sharpe's right? That you just trumped up an excuse for a little gentle bullying?"

The two were wisely silent.

"H'm," said Darrell thoughtfully. "You're both easily amused. If you want a set-to, why don't you pick on some fellow in the Fifth, who'd provide you with more fun for your money? A kid in the Third could lick Sharpe."

"We weren't going to hurt him," said Vidler.

Tallboys was toppled first into the blanket, to rise and fall in various ungainly postures.

47

"I may be mistaken," said Darrell, "but Sharpe didn't seem to want to be tossed in a blanket. So why not have left him alone?"

"We weren't going to hurt him!"

"In that case," said Darrell cheerfully, "how would you like to be tossed in a blanket? You were so keen on doing it to Sharpe, we'll see if you like it being done to you. Come on, you fellows," he called out to the rest of the dormitory, "bring a large blanket forward. We're going to toss Tallboys and Vidler in it."

The idea was hailed with joy. Tallboys and Vidler, the most unpopular couple in the middle and lower schools, were tolerated only on account of their size. There was no one else in the dormitory who had not suffered at their hands and did not jump at the chance of working off old scores. Only Tallboys and Vidler did not like the amended plan.

"You had better be quiet about it," said Darrell, "or I'll help the others scrag you before we toss you up. If I were you I'd submit and make the best of a bad bargain."

Tallboys was toppled first into the blanket,

to rise and fall in various ungainly postures. So great was the enthusiasm that twice he grazed the ceiling. Showers of plaster came down with him.

"That'll do," said Darrell, after a while. "Let him go. Now, you," turning to Vidler.

The first passenger was thrown gasping on to the nearest bed, and the second taken aboard to be treated in the same fashion.

"Now you others had better get into bed," said Darrell, "or you'll have a master snooping round. I'll be along myself shortly."

He departed, leaving the dormitory in almost unanimous high spirits. It was the general opinion that Darrell had responded nobly to the Situation. Here was a prefect after their own hearts—one who did not shirk his duties, but executed them in a highly entertaining manner. Moreover, he had shown them how to deal with Tallboys and Vidler, whose reign was thus brought to an end.

Darrell himself felt some satisfaction after this episode, for before going to bed he wrote to his father and told him about the prefecture.

Three days later he received a reply, express-ing parental astonishment and enclosing a one-pound note.

And on the evening of that day he moved into his new study.

CHAPTER V

MOVING IN—TUM, TUM

DEMANDS made on his time by the cricket captaincy prevented Darrell from moving in until near the end of the first week of term. Many things needed to be done, such as helping the secretary arrange fixtures for the First, Second, and Third Elevens with those of other schools, and arranging practices and trial games, and at the same time beginning his own practice at the nets.

Darrell's predecessor, Sims, was a brilliant cricketer who whilst still at school had hit up 104 for the Surrey Second against one of the minor counties. But Sims had shirked some of his duties, with the result that Darrell found a great deal to do.

Sims had fagged hard enough at getting the First Eleven into shape, but he had left the

Second Eleven almost entirely to the care of its captain, and about the Third Eleven and the fags he had not bothered himself at all.

This meant hard work for Darrell. Of last year's First Eleven only four remained—Darrell, Alfriston, Goulding, and Anstruther, Darrell's vice-captain. Thus the First Eleven was practically new, and the Second and Third Elevens required similar reorganization. The seven First Eleven recruits were Bennet, Kenton, O'Neill, Sutherland, Holmes, Denbigh, and Richmond. Darrell, unlike Sims, was not content to establish his fame on the record of the First Eleven only. He realized that to do so would not be of much use to Melhurst cricket, and that he must devote a good deal of energy to training the Third Eleven and the fags, upon whom the school would depend some time in the future.

Also, one or two reforms were needed in the system of coaching and practice. There were four cricket nets on the sports ground—one for each of the three elevens, and another for the fags. As various practice games were also always in progress, every one got a game of some sort. The fags, however, except for an occasional visit from the coach, were left very much to their own devices. Hardly an evening passed without a quarrel of some sort. Some one would declare that he should have his whack before some one else, who would at once declare that he jolly well shouldn't. Heated words would follow, a blow or two would be struck, and sometimes a free fight ensued. On one occasion the net came down on the participants during their efforts to kill one another as painfully as possible. A wriggling mass of fags was held in the strongly corded netting, some of which had to be cut away before they were released.

Darrell determined to alter all this. He issued an order whereby members of the First and Second Elevens had to take turns of twenty minutes in superintending and coaching the fags.

This order was not liked, but Darrell insisted on its being carried out. For the first time in his life he observed the advantage of discipline. Hitherto he had imagined himself merely directing and advising, but now he saw that advice and direction frequently needed a word of command to make them effective.

There was, for instance, the matter of early morning fielding. Darrell found that last year's Second Eleven players could be relied upon to stop a ball when it came straight for them, no matter how hard it was hit, but that if they had to dive or jump for it, more often than not they fumbled the ball. After a practice game one evening he said casually to the others :

" You might get up early to-morrow morning, you fellows, and come down and have some fielding practice before breakfast. I've seen penguins who can stop a ball better than most of you can."

" Does that apply to me ? " asked Kenton.

" It does."

" Well, I thought I could stop a ball as well as a penguin can. I may be mistaken, of course, but that's what I thought."

" I'm sorry to have to disillusion you," said Darrell. " You can't. But if you practise hard enough you might in time. Well, don't forget to-morrow morning about seven, will you, every one ? "

The next morning, Darrell, who was first out on the field, was soon joined by Anstruther and Alfriston, and the three whiled away the time waiting for the rest by throwing high catches up to one another.

" What a lot of slackers they are," said Darrell, when twenty minutes had gone by and no one else had appeared. " It'll be breakfast-time soon, and the morning'll have been practically wasted. Why on earth can't they be punctual ? "

The minutes ticked by, and soon Darrell realized that the absentees were not coming at all.

" This," said Darrell, approaching Anstruther and Alfriston, " is what I call enthusiasm. They really think they're good enough. And, honestly, there are some Second Eleven men— Larkin and Collinson, for instance—who are better at fielding than they are."

" They're a lazy lot," agreed Anstruther. " Wild horses wouldn't drag them out of bed half an hour earlier than usual."

" Well, I know what'll get them up whether

they like it or not. I'll put a notice on the board stating that their presence will be required at seven to-morrow. That'll be authoritative. They'll have to come down then."

The notice, when it was posted up, was not favourably regarded by those concerned. When Goulding read it he was particularly annoyed. He resented taking orders from Darrell, even about cricket, and he thought that Darrell was making a needless fuss over this question of early morning fielding.

" What's wrong with our fielding ? " he said to the others as they stood round the notice-board. " Hang it, I was in the First last year and Sims didn't say anything about it."

" The whole trouble with Darrell," grumbled Denbigh, " is that now he's cricket captain he feels his position, and he's going to get us up early just for the sake of it."

" That's what I think," agreed Bennet. " Darrell's getting swelled head. After all it would be different if we were really rotten fielders, but we're not. That's not bragging, it's the plain truth."

57

" He's altogether too fault-finding," said Holmes. " There was that drive of Goulding's the other day past me at cover. It was an impossible thing to get. I swear a county man couldn't have stopped it, and even though I tried, he grumbled because I missed the thing. He said I ought to shift more quickly than I do. Shift more quickly ! Good lord ! "

" Must we get up to-morrow, as he says ? " asked Kenton of Goulding.

" What d'you mean ? "

" Why, simply stay on in bed as if the notice wasn't on the board at all."

Goulding moved uncomfortably. " We can't very well do that. However much we dislike what he says, he's cricket captain, and supreme so far as cricket is concerned."

" You mean, then," said Kenton, " that he can get us up in the middle of the night for practice, if he wants to."

" Well, there are limits, of course. But early morning fielding isn't unknown. It's simply that we don't think he's justified in having it."

" So that's that," said Holmes. " We've got to do what the notice says. So it's not much use our grumbling."

With which philosophical summing up the group dispersed and went their separate ways.

At the appointed time the Eleven, some of them rubbing their eyes and yawning, turned out for the delayed practice. Early morning fielding was never popular, and to Darrell himself it was only a painful necessity. Most of the others were feeling surly, and so proceeded to throw the ball harder than was necessary. It was a silly enough way of letting off steam, but presently the ball was travelling from man to man with a terrific force.

Darrell was beginning to enjoy himself. Fielding practice conducted on these lines would soon bring up the standard of the team. He sent the ball very hard at close range to Goulding. Goulding sent it back still harder. The others took a rest and watched the pair apparently trying to kill each other in such an entertaining fashion. The thing had become a duel, with a cricket ball in place of swords or pistols. Darrell, although his hands were sore and tingling, could still see the funny side of it. He and Goulding must look awful fools, he thought, as he hurled the ball at the other's right foot. And a second later he put up his hand just in time to save his nose being broken.

Goulding, however, did not think it funny. But he, too, was determined not to be the first one to throw up the sponge.

Then he failed to get hold of the ball as it came low down on his right. An excruciating pain shot up his wrist, and he let out an " Ouch!" as the ball rolled to the ground.

" Sorry," said Darrell, hurrying to him. " Not hurt much, are you ? "

" No," said Goulding, nursing his hand.

It was a constrained party that broke up when the assembly bell rang.

That evening, while the prefects of Reed's House were settling down in their studies for some quiet intensive work, there came loud thumps on the stairs at the end of the corridor, and then the tramping of feet along the passage to Darrell's study. The prefects muttered to

themselves. Darrell was moving in with the
assistance of Larkin and Collinson.

" H'm, not bad on the whole," said Collinson,
as he inspected the room. " You'll be able to
give little supper parties to me and Larkin."

" How about to-night ? "

Collinson shook his head. " Sorry. We've
got too much work to do. There's one advantage you've got over us. You can go to
bed later. As it is, I'm afraid you'll be able to
avail yourself of our presence for only twenty
minutes."

" Well, let's get busy, then. It shouldn't
take us long."

Each study at Melhurst was provided with
a table, three chairs, a bookshelf, a desk, and
a strip of carpet. Unless you were a luxury-
lover you hadn't much furnishing to do on
your own account.

Larkin let fall a suitcase with a crash that
shook the floor.

" Here, steady on," said Darrell, " there are
fragile things in that."

" What ? Eggs ? "

" No, pictures and things."

He opened the suitcase and brought out a picture at which he gazed admiringly. " That's not bad, is it ? I scrounged it from Fowler in Lancaster's. He didn't seem to want it."

It was a lurid painting of a sunset in Cornwall. Waves, mountain - high, dashed themselves against grim, towering rocks. Sky, sea, and rocks were scarlet, as if the artist had meant to depict the Day of Judgment.

" A bit high, isn't it ? " inquired Larkin.

" That's why I got it. With Goulding so near I'll often be seeing red. Whenever I want to crack him over the head with a hammer, I shall simply come in here, have a good look at this picture, and feel better. Come on, you fellows. Let's get going."

The three began to move about the study putting articles in drawers, books on the shelf, and pictures on the walls, and while they were so engaged they made up a little song which went as follows :

Darrell, loudly : " I'm moving in, tum, tum ; I'm moving in."

Larkin and Collinson, equally loudly : " He's moving in, tum, tum ; he's moving in."

Darrell : " I'm moving in, tum, tum ; I'm moving in, tum, tum."

Larkin and Collinson : " He's moving in, tum, tum ; he's moving in."

Humphreys and Everton ground their teeth and said it was a bit thick. If Darrell behaved like this at the start, what would his conduct be like in the course of time ?

Goulding, on the other hand, listened with a cynical smile on his face. Such rowdyism was to be expected from Darrell. It was hard for the rest of the corridor, of course, but the Head must be obeyed. Oh yes, he must be obeyed.

The sound penetrated to Kenton's study on the Sixth Form corridor, and Kenton scowled. He himself would have had that study but for Darrell. As it was he had to be content with half a study—no, less than a half, for Grainger was big and fat, and would have found a railway station incommodious to live in.

About half an hour later Goulding happened to pass by Darrell's study. The noise had died down, and Larkin and Collinson had returned to their own quarters. Goulding stopped, arrested by a peculiar smell. He sniffed and almost reeled as he realized that Darrell was frying fish and chips. A wreath of blue smoke could be seen curling out of the keyhole of Study No. 12.

Suddenly, as Goulding stood there, the door was thrown open to reveal Darrell—Darrell in his shirt-sleeves, one hand holding a fork on which was impaled a fried chip. He had opened the window, but a blast of hot air fanned Goulding in the passage.

" I thought I heard some one," said Darrell. " Is there anything you want ? "

To Goulding he almost seemed to exhale blue smoke from his nostrils.

" No, nothing," gulped Goulding, as he turned on his heel and walked away.

There was no doubt about it, he thought, Darrell was common. What kind of a place could his home be ? He was lowering the whole tone of Melhurst. It was more than flesh and blood could stand.

Meanwhile Darrell was enjoying his supper, and musing as to whether Surrey could possibly beat Lancashire in the following week. Engrossed in this problem, he did not hear the door open, or know that some one was standing in the doorway, until he was startled by a discreet " Ahem ! "

Looking up, he saw a boy somewhat shorter than himself, with a large pair of glasses through which his eyes blinked nervously.

" Why, Curtis ! " said Darrell. " Come in ! "

CHAPTER VI

DARRELL RECEIVES A VISITOR

" I THOUGHT," said the new-comer, " that as we're next door to each other—I'm in Study 11, you know—I'd come in and see how you are."

" Thanks. You're the first prefect visitor I've had, and probably the last. Take a chair. Have some supper ? "

" Er—no, thanks. I've had mine."

Across Curtis's mind flashed the awful thought that Darrell might imagine he was trying to scrounge something to eat.

" Well," said Darrell, " and what's your opinion of this terrible state of affairs ? "

" What state of affairs ? "

" Why, my being shifted up among the elect. Don't you—by the way, how is it I haven't

66

seen you before, this term ? Where've you been ? "

" Oh, I only came back to-day. My sister had chicken-pox, and I had to stay at home in quarantine."

" Lucky man ! She's done her duty by you in the way a sister should. But in that case you haven't heard what's been going on this term ? "

" Humphreys told me a bit about it," admitted Curtis.

" I'll bet he did. Awful catastrophe. Yours truly planted on the prefects. Didn't he tell you how they went to the Head, and how it was all no good ? I was out of school at the time, but I heard about it afterwards."

Curtis laughed, and said, " Yes."

" The place has been seething with excitement," went on Darrell, " and the prefects are full of indignation. They don't seem to think that I might feel indignant too. I tell you frankly, I'd a jolly sight sooner be back on the Fifth Form corridor with Larkin and Collinson. Not," he added hastily, " that I've got anything against you. It's the others."

" I don't wonder at it," said Curtis sympathetically. " After all, I think they ought to have given you a trial before kicking about it. For all they know, you might become a model prefect. Not that that's much. But it can't have been very pleasant for you here this term. Has Goulding had much to say about it ? "

" Goulding ? Why, he's said so much about it that his face is altering from its usual bonny mould to that of a loud speaker. But for him the others wouldn't have been so bad. But with him as captain—oh, well, shall we leave the subject ? I suppose you haven't had much trouble moving in, Study 11 being yours last term."

" Well, I've still got some books and things to unpack. I think I'll go and get it over."

Darrell rose with him. " I'll come and help, shall I ? Oh, it's all right, I like it. If there's one thing I can do, it's unpack. When I leave school I think I'll get a job as a moving man, one of those fellows who wear green aprons."

They entered Study 11, and Darrell looked

around him approvingly. " By Jove, this isn't at all bad," he said.

For Curtis's study was quite agreeably furnished. Round the walls were hung good reproductions of masterpieces. There was an easy chair on either side of the fireplace, three or four shelves were filled with well-bound books, and the floor was adorned with a strip of carpet besides the one provided. A bowl of flowers stood on the table. Simple inexpensive things had been combined with skilful effect.

" By Jove," said Darrell again. This was the kind of study that he himself hoped to have when time and money permitted. He crossed to the shelves and examined the books.

" I see you've got the full set of Sherlock Holmes," he observed. " So have I. They're jolly good, aren't they ? "

" Rather ! They're better than all other detective stories."

Bending down, Curtis brought some books out of a box on the floor and piled them on the table.

" I say, what's this ? " asked Darrell, fingering the top of the pile.   " A photograph album ? "

" Yes."   Curtis laughed and reddened. " Family photographs and holiday views and things."

" May I have a look ? "

" If you want to."

Deeply interested, Darrell opened the volume. He had no prejudice against family albums. Indeed they had always provided him with interest and entertainment.

" Who's that ? " he asked, pointing to the photograph of a small girl perched on a fence.

" That's Jobyna, my sister."

" The one with small-pox ? "

" Chicken-pox.   I took that while we were on holiday.   Not bad, is it ? "

" H'm."   Darrell looked at it reflectively. " She looks a bit scraggy, though."

" Well, she is rather thin. But she'll get fatter in time, don't you think ? " Curtis asked anxiously, as though Darrell had power to prognosticate in this connection.

" Oh, I expect so. It's an old Spanish custom. Who's this fellow with the gun ? "

" That's my brother Jim. He was just going to pot a rabbit when I took it. The funny part about it was the baby broke away from Jobyna and toddled right in front of him just as he shot it."

" Poor kid ! What did they say at the inquest ? "

" Not the baby—the rabbit, I mean. It was his first one, and he didn't kill it outright. It made such an awful row before it was finally quietened that he vowed never to shoot anything again. And he hasn't done."

" It is a dirty business, killing things for sport, isn't it ? I always feel faintly sick when I think of it. Are these all photos of your family ? "

" Pretty nearly all. There are one or two views at the end. Go on, turn over. Now— there you are."

" Where did you take this ? " asked Darrell, examining a photograph intently.

" That's a view of the Downs near Eastbourne.

We spent last holidays there. Topping it was, too."

" I thought it was familiar. I live over Beachy Head way. Not very far, about two or three miles away."

" Good lord, I didn't know that. Funny I didn't see you, then. We spent close on six weeks there, and we were on the Downs nearly every day."

" I should be away myself at the time. We were in the north of France, not far from Wimereux. I didn't like it much. Country not half so good as the Downs. Are there any more views ? Why, here's one. I say, I know this well."

Darrell's heart had warmed to Curtis in the last few minutes. Life seemed to have taken a turn for the better. Praise of the South Downs could make of Darrell a friend for life.

He had always imagined Curtis, who was brilliant at his work and the holder of two or three scholarships, to be a kind of automaton existing merely to work out equations and translate Latin prose and verse. Now, however, he had found Curtis to be intelligent and amiable, and one who called the South Downs "topping." Darrell could have smacked Curtis on the back.

"I think we're going again for six weeks next year," said Curtis; "that is, if the guv'nor can get all that time off. He's a doctor, you know, but he doesn't care much for London. None of us do, in fact. He's thinking of trying to get a practice near Eastbourne."

"By Jove, it would be good if he did," said Darrell. "We'd see something of each other then. Lots of people say they wouldn't like to live there in the winter, but it's just as enjoyable as the summer. And, my hat, you can get some storms there now and again. Our house stands right by itself, and it fairly shakes when the wind whistles round Beachy Head. One night we had a winter thunderstorm, and I dressed and went out and watched it on Beachy Head. It was colossal. My people made rather a fuss about it when they found out. They said it was dangerous. But it was worth it."

"I'm hanged if I'd have done that. You might have fallen over the cliff."

" Oh, well, I didn't venture too near the edge. It's never wise to do that. The ground's so crumbly. No, my people seemed afraid that I might have been struck by lightning."

For some time they went on talking, until Darrell glanced at the clock.

" I say, it's half-past ten," he exclaimed. " I haven't kept you too long, have I ? "

" No, that's all right," said Curtis. " I've liked it."

" I'd better be toddling along to my dormitory." Darrell got up and moved slowly to the door. " We haven't done much unpacking, have we ? I'll come and help you with it to-morrow."

" Thanks. But I can do it myself, really."

" Well, I suppose I'll be seeing you in the form-room to-morrow."

" I don't know about that," said Curtis. " You see, Goulding, I, and a few others are allowed to work on our own to a great extent in the prefects' room. We're considered to be more advanced than the rest of the Sixth."

" Well, I'll still be seeing you somehow or other."

" Of course. So long ! "

" So long ! "

And in a minute the study was plunged into darkness.

CHAPTER VII

THE ODIOUS MR. CODY

DARRELL found in Curtis a friend who proved as entertaining in his way as Larkin and Collinson were in theirs. At the first favourable opportunity Darrell asked all three to tea together in his study. The occasion was a success.

"He's very different from what I expected. He's not a bit like the rest of the Sixth. Why, dash it, he's human," said Collinson of Curtis when the latter had left them.

Curtis, on his part, had plainly been entertained by Larkin and Collinson.

But whilst Darrell had made a new friend in Curtis, he had also discovered an enemy in the person of Mr. Cody.

Mr. Cody took the Sixth in mathematics,

and two or three other forms in physics. In the course of his scholastic career Darrell had managed to avoid physics. Forced at the age of thirteen to choose between the latter subject and Greek, he had chosen Greek largely because he did not like the look of Mr. Cody.

Mr. Cody was short, fat, and bald, with pale blue eyes, pendulous lips, and a sarcastic tongue. Also Mr. Cody was a snob—not one of those largely harmless snobs who respect only wealth and position, but the kind of snob who openly despises any one without these advantages.

A story was told at Melhurst about two boys whose names were Lemmin and Hamilton. Lemmin's father owned a house in Mayfair, a castle in Wales, a shooting-box in Scotland, and a villa on the Riviera. His income was rumoured to be so large that the tax imposed upon it was sufficient to pay for the upkeep of the army and navy. Lemmin Junior knew nothing, and was proud of the fact that he knew nothing. But this did not deter Mr. Cody from singling out Lemmin as his favourite. And in the end Mr. Cody was asked to spend part of his Christmas holidays at the Lemmin establishment in the south of France.

Hamilton's father was not so fortunately placed. He was a butcher in one of London's poorer localities, and his son had reached Melhurst by means of a scholarship. In the course of time this fact reached the ears of Mr. Cody, who immediately began a systematic persecution of Hamilton. Despite the fact that he was a brilliant scholar, the latter was harried and insulted at every opportunity. As Lemmin could do nothing wrong, so Hamilton could do nothing right. In the end he left, abandoning his intention of becoming a doctor, and went to help his father manage the shop.

And when Darrell came into the Sixth he found that he could no longer avoid Mr. Cody. And Mr. Cody, like Goulding and the prefects, considered Darrell fair game for measures of repression. Exuberance and unruliness were only justified in a boy whose parents were wealthy. And Mr. Cody had not forgotten the car in which Mr. Darrell had arrived for a school prize-giving a couple of terms before. It was a three-year-old Lorris, driven by Mr. Darrell himself.

For the first fortnight of the term Mr. Cody let Darrell alone. Then gradually he developed his attack. It was nothing much to begin with —merely a few pleasantries at Darrell's expense. Presently these quips took on a biting edge, and Mr. Cody began to find fault with Darrell upon every possible occasion, holding him up to ridicule by every means in his power.

Darrell's dislike of Mr. Cody rapidly grew into hatred, and on a day early in June the pair met in open battle.

At 11 a.m. Mr. Cody entered the Sixth Form room for an hour's algebra. Putting a pile of books down on his desk with a resounding thump, he turned to the blackboard and began wiping out a large map of Europe.

" This period we shall spend working out some problems together," he announced.

There was a perceptible brightening of faces. Forty boys working out one problem at a time was forty times less strenuous than forty boys labouring at forty individual problems. They leaned back in their chairs and waited.

Mr. Cody stood on his toes because he could not otherwise reach the top of the blackboard, and with much panting and puffing, for he was fat and the least exertion troubled him, wrote out the following :

" From 7 Englishmen and 4 Americans a committee of 6 is to be formed : in how many ways can this be done, (1) when the committee contains exactly 2 Americans, (2) at least 2 Americans."

Then he swung round and pointed a finger at Darrell.

" Tell us, Darrell," he commanded, " how to set about this."

Darrell, whose mind at the time was far away making out a cricket team for Reed's House against Lancaster's, endeavoured to collect his scattered faculties and concentrate on the more urgent problem at hand. He read through the writing on the board, and then read it again. After which he read it a third time.

"We are waiting, Darrell," Mr. Cody reminded him.

After reading the problem a fourth time Darrell had to confess himself beaten. He had not the slightest idea of how to arrive at a solution. In any case, one committee should suffice for any purpose. However, that was algebra all over.

"What formula are we to use?" inquired Mr. Cody.

"The one for quadratics, sir?" hazarded Darrell hopefully.

"Just so!" snapped the other. "One couldn't expect a more intelligent answer from you. Now have another try. Is there any other formula, it doesn't matter which, that you would care to give us just for the fun of the thing?"

Darrell pondered, and then replied:

"I'm afraid that's all I can do for you, sir."

The form sighed with ecstatic pleasure, and assumed the least uncomfortable positions possible on hard wooden seats. There might now be a scene, in which case not much algebra would be done this lesson.

Mr. Cody became ominously calm.

"Impertinence won't help you, Darrell," he said.

"I don't want it to help me, sir. There's no need."

"Your brain, I may take it, then, is sufficient to carry you unaided through an algebra lesson?"

"Hardly, sir."

"I'm glad you have the sense to admit it. But you needn't seem so proud of it. How d'you think you're going to get on if that's the case?"

"I shan't get on. I'm not rich enough, sir."

"Eh? What's that?"

"I haven't enough money to be good at mathematics, sir."

In the breathless hush which followed, Mr. Cody found it hard to believe his own ears. But having accepted their evidence, he pretended not to perceive the implication of Darrell's remark.

" What are you babbling about ? " he demanded.

" I'm not babbling, sir," was the quiet reply. " I'm just answering when you speak to me as best I can."

" Why not answer in a sensible manner, then ? "

" I am doing so, sir."

" I'm afraid you're the only one in this form who thinks so. Tell me, do you think you're an ornament among us all ? Eh ? Answer me ! "

This was a favourite question from Mr. Cody's repertoire. An answer in either sense could be used for purposes of ridicule.

" It wouldn't be difficult, sir," said Darrell, avoiding the double pitfall.

Mr. Cody glared, and the Sixth Form suddenly took a more personal interest in the fray.

Darrell's defiance seemed to include not only Mr. Cody. A resentful mutter went round the room, and Mr. Cody waited until it had subsided. Then he beckoned imperiously with a fat forefinger. " Come here ! " he commanded.

Darrell rose and confronted Mr. Cody before his desk.

Mr. Cody sat back in his chair and folded his arms on his bosom.

" You're not at all funny, Darrell."

" I know I'm not, sir."

There was a faint stress on the " I'm," too faint to give open cause for offence.

" Then why act like a fool ? "

" How, sir ? "

" Don't bandy words with me, Darrell. I've dealt with hundreds of boys in my time ; some have tried to get the better of me, but none has succeeded. Bear that in mind. Any more insolence from you and you'll look very sorry for yourself."

Darrell shook his head, and a faint smile curved the corners of his mouth.

" I never look sorry for myself, sir."

" Indeed ! And do you think that I am interested in your appearance ? "

" You've been very interested in me this term, sir. You haven't given me a moment's peace in class lately."

Pale with anger, Mr. Cody banged on the desk.

"Another word and I shall report you to Dr. Alcott. That will do."

"No, it won't do." Darrell was now speaking as loudly as Mr. Cody. "You've had your say, and I'm going to have mine. You can do what you like, you won't hurt me in the slightest. I'm not sensitive. You can't bully me as you bullied Hamilton. I'm only telling you this because you think you've been bothering me a lot this term. Well, you haven't. And now you can report me to Dr. Alcott if you like."

Mr. Cody pointed a quivering finger towards Darrell's vacant seat.

"Sit down!" he said thickly, imposing on himself all the restraint of which he was capable.

Darrell obeyed, and the tension in the room was relaxed. After flicking over the leaves of his book in a manner which was meant to be careless, but which did not deceive his form, Mr. Cody resumed the lesson, this time without the assistance of Darrell.

Mr. Cody was thoroughly disturbed by that allusion to Hamilton. He had had no idea that the Hamilton episode, almost forgotten by himself, had ever been discussed in the school with reference to his own part in it. His conscience stirred in that connection, and although he would have liked to punish Darrell, the matter might easily come before the Head, and Mr. Cody wanted no digging up of the past with Hamilton's name in it.

So for the present Mr. Cody determined to lie low. No doubt an opportunity would arise of making Darrell regret his insolence.

Mr. Cody wrote on the blackboard as if his chalk were dipped in Darrell's blood.

CHAPTER VIII

A GAME OF CRICKET AND A SPREAD

DARRELL forgot about Mr. Cody directly the lesson was over. He had the ability to dismiss unpleasant things from his mind, and except in mathematics classes he carried on as if Mr. Cody did not exist.

But the passage-of-arms was not forgotten by the rest of the Sixth. It was the subject of discussion in their studies for many a day afterwards, the general opinion being that Darrell had come out of it rather well. It was duly noted that Mr. Cody had not reported Darrell to the Head ; and many wild guesses were made at the reason for such surprising forbearance.

Darrell, meanwhile, was fully occupied with cricket. The First Eleven had so far done as well as could be desired. Their first match against St. John's College they had won by fifty-four runs, and their second match, against Beechurst, had been drawn, rain stopping a game that would certainly have resulted in a win for Melhurst. The Second and Third Elevens had also fared quite well.

But the First Eleven had done no better than Darrell had expected. Beechurst, usually a strong side, had this year sent a weaker team than usual, owing to an outbreak of chicken-pox in the upper school, and St. John's was always below the strength of Melhurst. The third match of the season would really test the strength of the First Eleven. This was an away match against Headley, who, with another school, Ferndale, were Melhurst's deadliest rivals. If Melhurst beat Headley, then they could reckon themselves a team to be respected. Last year, under Sims, they had done it, but in the two previous years this match had been lost.

" We ought to win," said Darrell to Anstruther the night before the match. " And, given our fair share of luck, I think we shall."

Anstruther nodded.

" Win the toss ; that's the thing. I've had a letter from a chap I know at Headley, and he says that one of their star bowlers, Coningsby, has suddenly left."

" Coningsby ?   Let me see, now," said Darrell thoughtfully.   " A little fellow with bushy hair, wasn't he ?   Oh yes, I know.   Well, that's all to the good.   Do they miss him much ? "

" You bet.   But they've still got Gray with them.   You remember him, don't you ? "

" When he made a hundred and three last time ?   I should think so.   That man's hot. When he's batting we'll have some fielding to do, I can tell you."

" I'm with you there," agreed Anstruther. " Our fellows must be extra slippy in the field."

" Fielding's not our strong point," Darrell admitted.   " We're not too bad, really, but then again we're not too good."

" Anyhow, win the toss," said Anstruther. " I always like to bowl at a side that's last in. And the wicket will give an advantage to the side that bats first."

Darrell did win the toss, and elected to bat first. Opening the innings with Alfriston, he scored a four off the first ball, a full toss on the leg, and the next one he hit for two. The Headley fast bowler had not yet found his length, and the first over realized ten runs.

After that, however, the scoring was by no means easy, the bowlers sending down balls that wanted watching all the way. At seventy Alfriston was caught at short leg, and at a hundred and ten Darrell was stumped in trying to hit a boundary off a deceptive googly, returning to the pavilion with fifty-five to his credit. Kenton, Goulding, and one or two others did their fair share towards raising the total, which had reached the two hundred mark when Anstruther, the last man but one, came in to bat.

And here an unpleasant surprise awaited the Headley team. Anstruther and Richmond maintained a stubborn defence, and raised the total by thirty-odd runs before Anstruther's wicket was spread-eagled by a yorker.

The final Melhurst score stood at two hundred and forty-one.

The opening pair for Headley played themselves in cautiously enough, the bowling being too good for them to take any risks. For the first half-hour the runs came slowly, but as their sight of the ball improved the two began to hit out. When the score stood at eighty-three Darrell tried a change of bowling, and at first this seemed successful. Getting too much under a ball, Gray, the more truculent of the two batsmen, drove hard in the direction of Goulding. Moving irresolutely sideways, Goulding fumbled the ball as it whizzed over his shoulder, juggled desperately with it, and dropped it. Amid a pregnant silence he threw the ball back to the bowler.

After that the score rapidly reached the hundred mark, and began to mount up still more rapidly towards the hundred and fifty.

Things were looking serious for Melhurst. Headley were now almost certain to force a win.

Then suddenly, hitting out at a ball which

rose more than he had expected, Gray was caught off Holmes, and his companion followed him, bowled, in the next over.

Now, as sometimes happens after a big stand in cricket, a rot set in. No less than three men were dismissed in the next over off Anstruther's bowling, and the over after that accounted for two more. From one Blades, however, the Melhurst bowlers met with a stubborn resistance, and he, in company with a stone-waller, revived the hopes of Headley. Between them the pair put on forty—they would only have made half this number if Denbigh had not missed a comparatively easy catch off Blades in the slips—before Blades was bowled. After that the result was a foregone conclusion. Melhurst won by forty runs.

Darrell, of course, could not be anything but pleased with the result. Melhurst had done well to beat Headley, and, except for their fielding, had shown themselves worthy opponents for Ferndale later on in the term. The fielding, whilst not really bad, had been inferior to that of the Headley team. Still, there was plenty of time for practice and improvement before the Ferndale match.

On the team's return to school Darrell was pounced upon by Larkin and Collinson, flushed by an easy victory of the Second over a local team.

" The Second Eleven and the Fifth are going to have a colossal tea in the Senior Common Room. Will you come ? " asked Larkin.

" Lord ! " said Darrell wistfully, " there's nothing more I'd like, but I've got too much to do."

" But aren't you going to have any tea ? " asked Collinson in amazement.

" I had a snack at Headley. I didn't eat much because I wasn't hungry."

" Well, come and have something, man. You needn't spend more than an hour on us."

Darrell shook his head. " It's no good, really. I've got too much to do. You'll have to get along without me."

" Well, if you won't, you won't," sighed

Collinson. "There'll be more grub for us, that's all."

"Have you got much grub?" inquired Darrell.

Collinson raised his eyes to heaven. "He asks if we've got much grub! Why, man, there's nothing we haven't got. There are doughnuts, sausage rolls, cream buns, cream horns, chocolate roll, swiss roll, jam tarts, meringues, Genoa cake, Madeira cake——"

"Stop!" said Darrell hoarsely. "Stop!"

"For drink," went on Collinson, "we've got ginger beer, lemonade, ginger ale, lemon squash——"

Darrell covered his ears with his hands and began to walk rapidly away.

"I say, Darrell!" Collinson shouted after him.

"What?"

"I'll tell you something we haven't got."

"What's that?"

"Bread and butter."

Darrell grinned to himself as he walked on. Those spreads that the Fifth held periodically, what fun they were ! Only a term ago he had been present, eating, drinking, laughing, talking with the rest. Now there was too much else waiting to be done.

In his study he turned this way and that, and his gaze fell on a large wooden cash-box standing in the centre of the table. He picked up the box and shook it. The contents jingled musically.

During the last few days Darrell had been collecting sixpence from each master and boy towards a large cricket spread given at the end of the term in the school hall. It now occurred to him that he had not yet approached the Fifth Form for their contributions. For a second he paused to stifle his conscience, knowing that once inside the Senior Common Room he would not be allowed to depart for some time.

Then he went quickly out, and in the passage met Curtis.

" I'm going to collect some money from the Fifth," he told him. " They've got a spread on, I believe," he added carelessly. " Coming ? "

Curtis grinned.

" You mean you're going to a spread, and might collect some money while you're there," he said. " All right, I'll come. But I can't spend long. I've got a lot of work on hand."

From Reed's House they crossed the quadrangle to the school buildings. As they drew near to the Senior Common Room a loud hum could be heard from within. Darrell threw open the door and stood surveying the occupants. The noise died down and rose again, this time with a note of welcome.

" Darrell, by Jove ! " said some one.

" Collinson and Larkin said you weren't coming," said another. " And here you are. You'll never get married ; you change your mind too quickly."

" Come on, Darrell ! " shouted a third. " Tell us what it's like being a prefect."

Darrell laughed.

" I've come to collect your money for the cricket spread," he announced, rattling his box.

" Cricket spread, my foot ! " said Collinson.

" Come and sit down. You, too, Curtis. Here are chairs for you both."

Darrell and Curtis wedged themselves in. Darrell was bombarded with questions. Was it true that the prefects drank bottled stout of an evening in the privacy of their studies ? Was it true that the prefects had found out that the Head had committed bigamy, even polygamy, and that he had sworn them to secrecy over it ? Was it true that Halisham, the school dandy, wore corsets, and hung them on the bed rail in the Sixth Form dormitory at night ?

Whilst he ate and drank and answered questions, Darrell looked about him with pleasure. This was like old times. The same pictures on the walls, the cracked mirror at the end of the room, the chairs with springs broken and protruding out of faded upholstery, were as friendly as the Fifth Formers themselves.

Mellish, an old acquaintance, looked across the table at him, smiled, and raised his glass of ginger beer.

" Cheerio, Darrell ! "

" Cheerio ! "

Time fled as if on wings. At seven Curtis slipped away, but Darrell could not bring himself to move. He sat fascinated by the sight and sound and atmosphere of the Fifth Form revelling in their spread.

Suddenly there was a lull in the noise, Larkin stood up, glass of ginger beer in hand, looking more woebegone than ever.

" In honour of the fact that we have a distinguished guest present," he announced, " in the shape of Darrell, once a member of this form, but now among the *élite*, I shall recite a well-known poem, ' Tha Tarch of Lafe,' bay Sar Henray Newbalt."

Larkin's voice had become and remained oppressively genteel as he carried out his threat :

" Thar's a braethless hash in the clawse to-nayt,
  Ten to meake and the metch to win,
  A bawmping peech and a bleending layt,
  An aor to plee and the lost mahn in. . . ."

Refreshing himself with sips of his ginger beer between verses, Larkin carried his burlesque to a triumphant conclusion.

Thees they all with a joyful maynd,
Beah through lafe lake a tarch in fleem,
And, fahling, fling to the hawst bahaynd
' Plee *ap*, plee *ap*, and plee the geem ! ' ''

The applause was deafening, rising and falling several times before it finally died down. In his enthusiasm Darrell continued to shake and jingle his cash-box.

" Here, how much have you got there ? " asked Wright, his neighbour, taking it from him.

" About six pounds ; all in sixpences."

" How d'you get at it ? "

" Pull out that little trap door at the bottom. But, I say, don't you do it. It'll all come out."

Darrell was too late. Wright had already " done it," and the contents rolled out on to the table in a large glistening heap.

" Treasure, by Jove ! " said Mellish. " Here, lemme have some."

There was a universal scramble to get in reach of the pile of sixpences. Darrell and Wright were flattened out by a mass of hurtling bodies. And in the midst of all this confusion and uproar, Mr. Cody walked softly into the room.

" On the ball ! " shouted Mellish.

" What's all this ? What's all this ? " boomed Collinson, as he reared his fat form on to Wright's shoulders.

" Help, I'm being crushed to death ! " came a muffled yell from Wright.

" I can't breathe," roared Darrell.

" Money, money, money ! " chanted Larkin.

Gradually the heap of bodies was somehow disentangled, and with starts and grunts and proddings Mr. Cody's presence was revealed to all. A silence fell, in which every one tried to appear unconcerned.

" Indeed ! " said Mr. Cody.

Outwardly embarrassed, Darrell and the others were inwardly indignant. What right, they asked themselves, had that fat little rotter to disturb them like this at the end of a meal ?

" Indeed ! " said Mr. Cody again, fixing his eye on Darrell. " A prefect taking part in this horseplay ! Whose is that money you were all scrambling for ? "

There was no answer.

"No one owns it?" Mr. Cody went on, raising his eyebrows.

"I'm in charge of it, sir," said Darrell. "It's the money I'm collecting for the cricket spread."

"And this is how you take charge of it? Well, perhaps you know no better. Put it all back in the box immediately."

Silently they complied.

"If there is any money missing, Darrell, I shall see that you make good the deficiency," said Mr. Cody. "If you must play about like a child of five with these companions of yours, kindly leave money which isn't your own in a safe place beforehand."

Darrell remained silent, with his eyes lowered.

"Do you hear me, Darrell?" asked Mr. Cody.

"Yes, sir."

"Excellent. Now let me give a word of warning to you all. The noise here could be heard all over the school buildings. It even reached me on the top landing. In the future behave more quietly if you want to keep out of detention. Remember that there are others about to whom quiet is valuable. Try to be less selfish and childish."

With that Mr. Cody withdrew.

"What business was it of his what we were doing?" asked Wright. "Another master wouldn't have said anything."

"Another master wouldn't have come in at all," Darrell told him. "I say, it's getting late. You fellows have got your prep to do, and so have I. I'd better be going."

Darrell was not the only one to be making a move. There was the restless shuffling of feet and sound of smothered yawns which always heralds the breaking-up of a party.

"We're coming too," said Larkin. "Stretch yourself, Collinson."

"Come again, Darrell," said Mellish. "We don't see much of you now."

"I will. So long!"

"So long!"

CHAPTER IX

AT THREE O'CLOCK IN THE MORNING

"YOU know," said Collinson, as he kept up with Darrell's long strides across the quadrangle, "the more one gets to know of Cody the more repulsive he seems."

"Not with me," said Darrell. "He seemed to me as repulsive as possible when I first came here. He reached the limit then."

"It would happen," ruminated Collinson, "that a man like that should be in a position to wield power over others. I expect he decided when very young to be a schoolmaster, so that he could spend his life giving rein to a vindictive nature."

"He fairly loves putting the wind up the younger kids," said Larkin. "Do you remember, Collinson, how when we were fags he made our lives a misery ? Have you noticed how when he comes into a room all the chaps who see him go quiet ? Well, he fairly revels in that. You can see him enjoying it."

" He's certainly got a diseased mind," said Larkin, stopping suddenly. " Look at this, for instance."

In one corner the school quadrangle was bordered by the small garden of Mr. Cody's house. Mr. Cody was one of the few masters at Melhurst who boarded by themselves. His garden, although of course out of bounds for the boys, was fenced off not by railings or woodwork of any description, but only by a row of bushes.

Now Mr. Cody had ornamented an otherwise pleasant garden with a statue, on the base of which was the inscription " Julius Cæsar." The sculptor was perhaps merely experimenting, or taking skilful advantage of a current boom in the grotesque ; or he may have been expressing in stone the soul-form of a dictator. At all events he had made of Julius Cæsar a grim yet idiotic monster, whose outstretched arm ended in an eagle's talon, and whose legs were thickened like tree-trunks.

This statue, displayed in a London exhibition, had stirred some instinct in Mr. Cody. Professing artistically to admire it, Mr. Cody bought the statue and set it up in his garden, to the horror of the other masters and the amusement of the boys. Even the tolerant Dr. Alcott made a detour round the quadrangle rather than pass Mr. Cody's statue.

" It makes me go cold inside," said Darrell. " As if I'd had too many ice-creams."

" Julius Cæsar, by Jove ! " growled Collinson. " I wonder if any others were like that in his time."

" If so, no wonder they wore togas," Darrell pointed out. " What would they have looked like in modern costume ? "

" Bowler hat, trousers, and a walking-stick, what ! " said Larkin. " I——"

He broke off and turned to the other two, his usually solemn face transformed by a gleam of excitement.

" I say, I've got an idea."

" Where ? " asked Collinson.

" What about breaking out of school to-night and dressing Julius up ?   I've got an aged pair of trousers that we could slit up and tie round the legs. We could get that one arm into a coat sleeve, and Collinson's got that frightful bowler he wore in the play last term."

Darrell and Collinson regarded Larkin with approval.

" Marvellous ! " said Darrell at length.

" The very idea ! " breathed Collinson.

" How shall we get out ? " asked Larkin. " The same way as before ? "

" Of course. You two bring the props, wrapped up so that they'll be easy to handle, and I'll meet you on the first-floor landing at the back at—well, let me see now. We want to get some sleep as well. It's no use going to bed again and only having a couple of hours before we have to get up. Let's say three o'clock. We'll get out of the window over the lobby. It's easy enough to reach the ground from that low lobby roof. We can't get into the quad-rangle through a ground-floor window, as all the ground-floor rooms are locked up at night, and all the passage windows are barred. We get back the same way, of course. Is that clear?"

"Yes," said Larkin and Collinson together.

"Three o'clock," repeated the latter. "We'll be there."

"And don't forget the clothes. You'd better——"

"I say," interrupted Collinson, "do you realize that we've been discussing this thing almost on the blighter's doorstep? He may be watching us at this minute."

"No," said Darrell. "There's a masters' meeting up at school now."

"Oh, good! But there's another thing. Where's his bedroom? If it's round this side we're running a frightful risk."

"It isn't. It's round the other side, over-looking the playing fields. I know, because once in a practice match I hit a ball clean through the window, and he came out on the field there and then, blue with rage, to tell me that I'd smashed his water-jug. Can you imagine what the fellows'll say when they see his old statue all dolled up ? As for Cody, he'll be as wild as a cat on hot bricks."

" Here, but supposing he sees it to-morrow morning before any one else does ? " objected Larkin.

" That'll be all right," said Collinson. " Cody is never out of his house before breakfast-time. There's absolutely no flaw in the scheme. It's an idea in a million, and I say here and now——"

But Darrell cut him short by grabbing at his arm.

" Do you realize it's eight o'clock and we haven't even started our prep ? "

Row by row the lights of the school went out, until only masters' windows glowed singly here and there. Presently these too grew black, and for a while the school clock chimed away the hours of darkness. Some time after mid-night a half moon got up, silvery white amid scurrying cloud-rack, for now a stiff breeze was blowing.

Three o'clock struck, and Darrell opened the door of his dormitory. Carrying his shoes in his hand, he crept down to the first floor of the house. Presently he was joined by the dim shapes of Larkin and Collinson, the former carrying a large parcel.

" Got everything there ? " whispered Darrell.

" You bet," Larkin whispered back. " And we've brought some crayons to give the face a bit of colour."

" Good business ! "

" I say ! " muttered Collinson.

" What's the matter ? "

" The window over the lobby is open already."

" Good lord, so it is ! "

Above the sill of the open window tendrils of ivy waved in the breeze.

" Roberts, the porter, must have been slacking to-night," said Darrell.

" I'll get through first," said Larkin. " Then when I'm on the ground one of you drop the parcel to me from the roof of the lobby."

He climbed out of the window and made his way down the drain-pipe on to the roof of the lobby. Collinson, agile in spite of his size, went next, and when he had reached the lobby roof Darrell dropped the parcel to him, and he in turn dropped it to Larkin, who by now was on the ground. In a minute or two all three were in the quadrangle together.

"Now !" said Darrell. "Come on !"

For the moment no clouds were passing over the moon. The three adventurers hugged the shadow of the buildings, working their way in the direction of Mr. Cody's house. Once or twice they had to dart across a moonlit space, and when they reached Mr. Cody's garden only the bushes gave them any shelter.

"We'll have to look jolly slippy," said Darrell. "There's no shadow to hide us here; it's almost like daylight."

Larkin fumbled at the parcel.

"What's the matter with the thing ?" he grumbled. "It would——"

"Not so loud," murmured Darrell. "Here, I'll do it for you."

He took out a clasp-knife and cut the string. Then he turned to survey the statue, standing white and grotesque above them.

" I'd better dress and rouge him," he said. " I'm tallest. Give me a back, Collinson. You can hand the things up when I want 'em, Larkin."

He climbed on to Collinson's back, and stood staring at the statue with one hand on its shoulder to steady himself.

" Golly ! " he murmured. " I'll have a nightmare when I get back to bed."

Then he held out a hand in the direction of Larkin.

" Give me the hat first," he said. " Come on, man, what's the matter with you ? "

Glancing round, he saw Larkin staring open-mouthed in the opposite direction.

" What is it ? " he whispered.

" Look, over there ! A fellow getting on to the lobby roof ! "

Darrell gazed hard and nearly whistled.

" By Jove, yes ! " he observed.

He jumped down from Collinson's back, and all three watched the distant figure climbing by the means they had used for their descent.

" I wonder who it is," said Darrell. " I say, he's seen us."

The figure was now upright on the roof, and apparently staring in their direction.

" I'm going to see who it is," said Larkin, and before the other two could speak he made rapidly off across the moonlit quadrangle. At once the figure on the roof turned and began to move slowly up the face of the house, obviously by means of the drain-pipe. Evidently he did not mean Larkin to discover his identity.

And by the time Larkin reached the shadow of Reed's House the climbing figure was disappearing through the open window. Darrell and Collinson stood staring, and presently Larkin reappeared, coming back towards them. This time he used more caution, but still he ran quickly, and was soon once more beside the statue.

" Well ? " inquired Darrell.

Larkin shook his head, too puffed to speak for a second or two.

" I couldn't see who it was," he gasped. " Only that he was big enough for a Sixth

Former. But he's a dirty rotter, whoever he is. He's shut and latched the window."

" What ? " muttered Darrell and Collinson together.

" He's gone and shut and latched that open window," said Larkin.

CHAPTER X

MONEY, MONEY !

"BUT how d'you know he latched it ? He may only have shut it," said Darrell.

"I saw his hand move against the window-pane, and heard the latch squeak as he did it. He kept his other hand over his face so that I shouldn't see who he was."

Darrell took a deep breath.

"Well, I'm hanged. Why on earth should he do that ? What a swine to shop us on purpose ! "

They stared at one another in dismay, dis-missing all thought of the statue. Here they were, locked out of their house, with no means of entry short of ringing the bell and summon-ing their housemaster, Mr. Sparrow, to open the door for them. If they stayed outside all night, one of the porters would find them and

report them. That would be a scurvy ending
to what had been a promising adventure.

At last Darrell spoke.

" Well, we'd better get back to house before
we decide what to do," he said. " Have you
got the clothes, Larkin ? We don't want to
leave those lying about ? "

Dejectedly they regained the shadow of Reed's
House. The only windows now open, so far
as they could see, were those of the bedrooms
on the top floor.

" Are you sure he latched it ? " whispered
Collinson.

" I'm absolutely positive."

" Well, I'll tell you what we'd better do
first," muttered Darrell. " Let's go round the
house and see if any first-floor windows are
open. It's just worth trying."

" Roberts isn't likely to have left another
window open," objected Collinson.

" I don't believe he left that one open. That
blighter we saw must have opened it on his
way out before us. If you ask me, he'd been
off the school premises. We only spotted him

when he reached the house. We didn't meet him in the quadrangle. He must have come round by the chapel. You know that bit of the school wall over the lane there. It's crumbled away on top and easy to get over."

" That's what I think," said Larkin.

" Well, you two go this way, and I'll go that. Roberts often goes to bed before some of the masters, so he may not have been round all their rooms."

A few minutes later Darrell again confronted his dejected allies.

" We're in luck," he told them. " Old Tweet-tweet's gone and left his study window open."

" Colossal luck ! " breathed Collinson.

" It'll be rather hard to get at. Still, we ought to manage it. Come on ! "

Mr. Sparrow's window was about twenty feet from the ground. Ten feet from the ground was a ledge, about six inches broad, that ran the length of the wall. This and the creeper were their sole means of climbing up the wall.

"Hope the ivy won't give way under me," murmured Collinson.

"Oh, it's pretty strong stuff," said Darrell. "Old Wilkins once climbed all the way down from the second storey of Reed's House, using only the creeper, and won a bet of five bob. He was jolly hefty, too. I'll go first. You throw the parcel up to me when I tell you, Larkin."

Catching hold of a stem of ivy, he swung himself slowly up, testing each foothold with care, and pulling hard at each branch before he rested his weight on it. By this means he reached the ledge, and after climbing a few more feet found he was able to grip the sill of the open window. Safely inside, he held out his hands and Larkin threw the parcel up to him. Collinson and Larkin followed without mishap.

And there, in Mr. Sparrow's study, they rested for a few minutes, marvelling at their escape. The school clock struck four. They had only been out for an hour.

"I shall never break out of school again," Collinson whispered at length. "This has just about shattered my nerve. I swear my hair will be grey to-morrow."

" It was a bit sticky," agreed Darrell.

" I want to know," said Larkin savagely, " who the swine was who tried to do us down."

" And then I'd like half an hour with him," said Darrell. " Well, we'd better leave all the talking about it till to-morrow. I'm off to bed."

At the end of the passage they separated.

" Good-night, you fellows," whispered Darrell. " Pleasant dreams if possible."

" Good-night ! "

But Darrell himself was unable at once to go to sleep. Who on earth, he wondered, could that other adventurer be ? Why on earth should any one have wanted to play such a dirty trick ? The more he thought about it the more confused he became. And at length weariness overtook him. He left off worrying and drifted into sleep.

" And he held his hand over his face ? " said Curtis in amazement.

" Right over his face ! " said Larkin.

Thoughtfully Curtis kicked a stone in the direction in which they were walking. At that hour, just after dinner, the quadrangle was crowded with boys taking a stroll before the afternoon's work.

" Of what build was he ? " asked Curtis. " You've only told me he was tall. Was he thin or hefty ? "

" Just about medium," said Larkin. " It's impossible to say any more than that."

" And neither of you two saw him distinctly ? " turning to Darrell and Collinson.

" Only at a distance," said Darrell. " Just a dim shape, that's all."

" Worse luck ! " added Collinson. " But for old Tweet-tweet's window being open we'd be for it to-day, and no mistake."

" He must have known who *you* were. How was that if you didn't recognize him ? "

" Well, it would be fairly easy to spot Collinson a long way off. Also, he probably recognized Larkin when Larkin ran towards him. And it wouldn't take Sherlock Holmes to deduce that where Larkin and Collinson are, I can be found too. But I give the thing up. I don't want to talk about it. I only know that if ever I find out who the fellow is I'll make things pretty hot for him."

" I bet he's surprised to see us walking round this morning as if nothing had happened," said Collinson, with a grin. " He's probably making himself dizzy wondering how we got in."

" Are you still going to dress up old Cody's statue ? " asked Curtis.

" Not for some time, anyhow," said Darrell, yawning. " We've lost one beauty sleep already and had enough of night operations for some time."

" And this morning fellows might have been bursting at the way we'd improved Julius Cæsar," groaned Collinson.

" Well, it might have been a darn sight worse," said Larkin. " You, at this moment, might be bending over a chair in the Head's study—he's always got more power to his stroke just after dinner. How would you like that ? "

" Oh, give the thing a rest," said Darrell. " Well, what do you want ? "

This last remark was addressed to a small boy with a face rather like that of a Pekinese, who stood barring his way.

" Please," he said to Darrell, " the Head wants you."

" What for, do you know ? "

" No. He said he just wanted to see you, and as I was in his study at the time about a letter my father had written him—I want to know if I can go home a day earlier at the end of the term, because my father's going abroad on business then, and I'm going with him— he sent me to find you, and I looked for you in your study, but I couldn't find you, so I went to Mr. Sparrow and he told me to look for you down here, and so I came down to tell you that the Head told me that——"

" All right, all right. You ought to be an M.P. Cut along ! "

He turned an anxious face to the others.

" You don't think he's found out——"

" Who's talking about it now ? " demanded Collinson triumphantly.

" I don't see how he can have done," said

Larkin. "Anyhow, *you*'d better cut along too."

"All right. So long! Bear up meanwhile."

Darrell's fears were soon dispelled. The Head, as it turned out, wanted him on quite a trivial matter.

"About that money for the cricket tea, Darrell," he said. "I shall require it by to-morrow. It's ready, isn't it ?"

"I've still got the Sixth to collect from, sir. But I can soon do that."

"Very well. Bring it to me to-morrow morning directly after assembly."

"Yes, sir."

On his way to the prefects' room in the school buildings, where he now found it most convenient to keep his cash-box and the register that went with it, Darrell passed Larkin and Collinson. Their anxious expressions vanished as he grinned and shook his head.

Most of the Sixth were in their form room, awaiting the beginning of afternoon school.

"Money, please, everybody," he said. "The Head wants it all in to-morrow."

As he received each sixpence he ticked off the subscriber's name. Only a few of the prefects were present, and Darrell resolved to visit the rest that evening after tea. When he entered the prefects' room he noticed that the window was broken right across.

" Who did that ? " he inquired.

" Young Ballantyne, with a ball," growled Everton. " He knew it was forbidden to play with a cricket ball in the quadrangle. We've just had him up here and given him a tanning."

" It looks as if we've had a binge. The fellows'll be asking us where we keep the drink."

" We'll leave you to answer them," said Goulding.

" All right. I will. I'll say you keep it in your locker. Can I have your cricket tea money now ? "

Soon afterwards the others left the room, and Darrell settled down to check his grand total. Satisfied that it was correct, he left the box on his own table and went back to his study.

The next morning, after assembly, he followed

the Head to the latter's study, taking with him both cash-box and register.

" Now, Darrell," said the Head, taking off his gown and throwing it on the back of a chair, " let us check this together before you go. You have already checked it once, I presume."

" Yes. Last night, sir. It worked out all right."

" Good. Then we shouldn't have much trouble with it now."

The Head sat down at his desk and took the register and cash-box.

" You can't have collected from every one, of course. A few boys are always absent for one reason or another."

" Yes, sir. I've put a cross against the names of those who are in the sickroom."

" So I see. Now, how do you open this box of yours ? "

" Pull out that trap-door at the bottom, sir."

" Ah, yes. I must be careful that none of the money falls on the floor. It would be rather——"

As he emptied the contents of the box on

his desk the Head's voice tailed off into silence. Darrell gave a gasp of astonishment.

For instead of a stream of shining sixpences there poured out of the box some hundreds of pieces of tin of the same size. Lustreless in the bright sunshine, they lay on the Head's desk.

CHAPTER XI

"SOME BOY IN THIS SCHOOL . . ."

DARRELL never remembered that moment without an inward shudder. For what seemed an age he and the Head stared down at the heaped-up pieces of tin. Darrell's face went red and then pale. The noise made by a group of boys crossing the quadrangle came to him as if from another world. The Head sat as if turned to stone, except that the pulse beat visibly at his temple.

At last Dr. Alcott looked up at Darrell, and any doubts he might have had as to the boy's part in this affair were dispelled by the sight of Darrell's face.

"You know nothing about this, Darrell?" he asked.

"Nothing at all, sir."

"And you checked the money last night?"

" In the prefects' room."

" At about what time ? "

" Between ten and half-past."

" That was just before going to bed, then ? "

" Yes, sir. I was the last to leave the room."

" And did you leave the box there ? "

" Yes, sir. When I haven't got it with me I keep the box on my table in the prefects' room."

" Then the money must have been taken and these pieces of tin substituted during the night."

" Yes, sir."

The Head ran his hand through the heap of tin pieces.

" Either some one intends this as a joke, or the money has been stolen. But in either case I do not understand how the culprit managed to break into the prefects' room. All the ground-floor doors and windows in the school itself are locked for the night. Unless, of course, you were careless in not seeing that the window was properly latched, and unless one of the porters was equally careless in not examining it. Even then it is hardly credible that any one should break out of his house at night on the chance of effecting an entrance to the prefects' room."

And then another thought occurred to the Head.

" Of course," he went on slowly, " it might have been one of the prefects themselves. Everybody is under suspicion in an affair of this sort. If it is a joke, then I should look for the joker among the middle forms. In that part of the school boys have cast off the timidity of the junior and not yet acquired the responsibility of the senior. If it is not a joke, I should expect to find the culprit among the middle forms or seniors."

" There's something I've just remembered, sir," put in Darrell.

" What is that ? "

" That the window in the prefects' room was smashed yesterday by a junior playing about in the quadrangle with a cricket ball. So, well, couldn't it have been an ordinary burglar or a stray tramp who broke in, or—well, the servants have seen the broken window."

" Ah ! by solving one difficulty you have brought forward another. Now, do you know if anything besides the money has been missed from the prefects' room ? "

Darrell thought rapidly.

" I don't think so, sir," he said at length. " I left a bag of cakes on my table last night, and it was there this morning. Also, Goulding's got an expensive silver inkstand that he left in the prefects' room, and he was using it this morning."

" A servant or a burglar would have taken these things as well. And a burglar or a tramp would have broken into other rooms, and he would not have substituted this tin for the money."

" And none of the servants would know that I've been collecting the money," said Darrell.

" There's another thing, you see. By the way, was it known amongst the boys that you kept this box in the prefects' room and not in your study ? "

" Pretty well known, sir. Often fellows would come up to me with their money for the spread when I hadn't got my cash-box with me, and so I left it in the prefects' room, where they could go and put their money in the box and make a tick against their names in the register. That was always more convenient for them than fagging over to Reed's House, and besides, I didn't want a lot of fellows tramping in and out of my study."

"There's just one thing more. Was it known that I should require the money to-day?"

"I think so, sir. I told quite a lot of fellows that you did."

"So that the boy, whoever he is, seized the opportunity afforded him by the broken window to substitute these pieces of tin for the money during the night. It was certainly very ingenious. No one would guess by shaking the box that there was not real money inside it."

"It took me in, anyhow, sir."

"Well, Darrell," said the Head, in the tone of one who has made up his mind, "let us hope that it is merely a joke played by some one with a misguided sense of humour. If that is so, I shall find out to-morrow morning in assembly. Meanwhile, you will oblige me by telling *no one* about this affair. I prefer to communicate it to the school myself. Is that clear ? "

" Yes, sir."

" You can go to your form room now, and— I think you'd better leave this curious collection with me."

" Very well, sir."

Once outside the door Darrell blinked and shook himself.

" Well, I'm jiggered," he muttered. " Abso . . . bally . . . lutely jiggered."

" Some boy in this school is either an idiot or a thief."

The school assembly froze to silent immobility. One boy, about to scratch his head, kept his hand half raised, the forefinger crooked ready to scratch ; another had his face wrinkled up preparatory to blowing his nose, and he kept his handkerchief in place and his face tight in its wrinkles ; a third leaned forward in his chair staring fixedly at a pin with which he had been about to prick the boy in front of him.

Even the Head could not have desired a more dramatic response to his words ; and it was almost with a start that he himself spoke again. Beginning with the tale of how Darrell had checked the accounts in the prefects' room before going to bed, he next described how he himself had opened the cash-box, to find tin instead of money, and explained why he believed the substitution must have been effected by a boy in the school.

The school listened with bated breath.

"And now," said the Head, "I am going to see whether this is the work of a practical joker or a thief."

He took out his watch and placed it on the desk before him.

"I am going to allow one minute to elapse, and if by the end of that time no boy has come forward with a frank confession, we shall know that we have to deal with a thief."

The seconds ticked quickly by. The Head stood erect with arms folded and eyes searching

the ranks before him.   Again a frozen silence
gripped the boys ; through the open windows
a light breeze carried the distant lowing of
cattle and the near-by conversation and laughter
of two porters from the cloisters.

Suddenly the Head took up his watch, closed
it with an audible snap, and put it in his pocket.

" Very well," he said quietly.   " Let us not
beat about the bush.   There is a thief amongst
us."

There was a faint stir in the hall.   Boys sighed,
cleared their throats, and leaned back in their
chairs.

" I do not mind admitting," the Head went
on, " that there is very little likelihood of his
being discovered and exposed.   All of you know
it to be a disgrace that a school renowned and
honoured throughout England should count
among its pupils a thief.   For the sake of Melhurst, and for the sake of all those of you who
are innocent, I earnestly hope that this wretched
boy will be found and proved to be guilty.   If
he is found he will be expelled.

" You will have to bear among you the

monetary loss, which of itself is no great matter. To a certain extent this loss was due to Darrell's carelessness in leaving the cash-box overnight in the prefects' room with the window broken. However, we cannot blame Darrell for taking it for granted that the money would be safe. No one else might have done otherwise. The money will have to be collected again in due course.

" That is all for the present. I shall do everything in my power to find out who is the thief.

" School, dismiss ! "

The effect of the incident on the school was largely one of pleasurable excitement. Who was the thief ? He might be one's own best friend. This was an Edgar Wallace thriller brought to life. The more innocent any one seemed, the more likely he was to be guilty. Boys would find themselves confronted by others who said persuasively : " Now, come on, old man, be frank and own up. It was you, wasn't it ? " Small boys were pounced on by bigger boys, who threatened that if they didn't own up it would go jolly hard with them. And one unfortunate, whose father was a Socialist Member of Parliament, was hounded round the quadrangle by a crowd of about fifty, who shouted, " You did it. You know you did. You thought it was Socialism."

Of course, not a few became amateur detectives, and spent hours outside the prefects' window lying flat on the ground, with magnifying glasses in hand, or walking round in circles with intent expressions on their faces. One wag turned up in a dressing-gown, with a pipe in his mouth, and leading a seedy-looking bloodhound borrowed from some one in the village. According to him, all the bloodhound had to do was sniff round the window and make straight for the thief. The bloodhound did sniff round beneath the window, and then loped off in the direction of Mr. Cody's house. . . .

Most of the school felt quite agreeably disposed towards the thief. This excitement was felt to be worth the extra sixpence which it had cost.

But when the first wave of excitement had

passed, another less pleasant feeling spread through the school.

One day, about a week after the memorable assembly, Darrell went to find Denbigh and tell him about an alteration in the supervision of junior practice games. At last he espied him across the almost deserted quadrangle.

" Hi, Denbigh ! " he shouted.

Denbigh turned, looked straight in his direction, then walked on as if he had not heard.

" Denbigh ! I say, Denbigh ! " called Darrell again.

Unheeding, Denbigh passed on and disappeared round by the cloisters.

" Well, I'm blest ! " said Darrell blankly. " What's the matter with the man ? Is he deaf ? "

Two boys from Segal's came by at that moment, and he turned to them.

" I say, Norman, and you, too, Gerard, d'you know if there's anything up with Denbigh ? I swear he deliberately ignored me just now."

"D'you still say that about Darrell?   Eh, Crowle, you swine?"

For a moment they stopped, evidently embarrassed, and then, to his astonishment, turned and walked on as Denbigh had done.

Darrell stared after them, amazed and then angry.

" What on earth's the matter with them ? " he demanded. " Have all three gone crazy ? "

Giving up the puzzle with a shrug of his shoulders, he turned and walked back towards Reed's House. As he neared it he saw Collinson sitting on the chest of a recumbent figure. Collinson was splashing water from a puddle into the face of his supine victim.

" And even now you're not half so filthy outside as you are in," Collinson was saying. " D'you still say that about Darrell ? Eh, Crowle, you swine ? "

" Ow, ow, ow ! " panted Crowle.

" Do you ? " went on Collinson, remorselessly flicking water.

" Stoppit, you rotter. You wait, Collinson. I'll——"

" I can keep on at this for hours if need be," said Collinson. " Come on, now. Be sensible.

Are you still going on saying that about Darrell ? "

" Ow, no ! "

" You promise not to breathe it to another living soul ? "

" Yes. I promise ! "

Collinson rose, hauled the other to his feet, and booted him hard three times.

" Now, get ! " he commanded.

Crowle " got."

Then Collinson turned to find himself confronted by Darrell. There was an instant's pause.

" Hallo ! " said Collinson, rather feebly.

" What was it that Crowle was saying about me ? " inquired Darrell.

" Oh, nothing."

" Come on, tell me."

" Nothing, really."

" Look here, Collinson, don't rot. There must be something. And I bet it's mixed up with something that's just happened to me, too." Darrell recounted how he had been ignored by Denbigh, Norman, and Gerard.

"Now, you must tell me," he said. "After all, if it's about me I've got a right to know."

"Well, it's like this," said Collinson hesitatingly.

"Go on !"

Collinson plunged.

"The fellows are saying that you're the thief."

CHAPTER XII

ELECTRICITY IN THE AIR

"THAT I'm the thief?" repeated Darrell. Then, as he understood, he added, "Good lord, what rot!"

"Of course it's rot. But that's what they say."

"Who are 'they'?"

"The fellows. You know how things get about."

"D'you really mean to tell me that everybody's saying I'm a thief?"

"Lord, no! Lots simply refuse to believe it. But there are some who do believe it."

"Why hasn't this reached me before?"

"You'd be the last person to hear it, seeing it's about you. I only got it myself the day before yesterday. Of course, I've stamped on it as much as I can. So has Larkin."

"But I can't get this thing right," said Darrell.

" Why should it be thought I did it rather than any one else ? Why should I have broken into the prefects' room in particular ? "

" They're not saying that you broke in. Look here, this is the rumour. Who is likely to have taken the risk of breaking out of his house to steal that money ? You can't really think of any one, can you ? Very well, how did the money go ? You were in charge of it. So what could have been easier than for you to have pinched the money yourself, probably in your own study, and then have substituted those bits of tin, and let the Head find it out himself when you gave him the box ? Naturally he would never have suspected you. But lots of fellows are asking what else there is to believe."

" Well, I'm blest ! What could I do with all those sixpences ? "

" You could change them somewhere. Some one else has evidently found a use for them."

" Yes, I suppose so. And, hang it, if they choose to believe that I took the money, how can I prove that I didn't ? "

" This is enough proof as far as I'm concerned," said Collinson grimly, shaking his clenched fist. "Just let them say it when I'm about. Mind you, none of the Fifth believe it. They know you too well."

"That's something, anyhow," said Darrell slowly. "Hallo, here's Curtis and Larkin. I've just been hearing this rumour about yours truly," he told them when they approached. "Previous to which I was cut dead by three fellows."

"Oh, you mean that—that——" Curtis floundered rather helplessly.

"That I'm a thief," grinned Darrell cheerfully. "Don't mind me."

"It's all rot, of course," said Larkin.

"So Collinson said. But a lot of fellows don't seem to think so. Is there a general move on to cut me?"

"Only amongst a few," said Larkin. "Mostly among fellows like Denbigh and Richmond. You know, that crew."

"Yes, I know. Let me see now, what's the time? Half-past five. Tea's just about ended. I'm going along to the Senior Common

Room to see how many fellows really believe this about me there. It'll be rather crowded now. Coming ? "

" Right-o ! " said Curtis.

They drifted away.

The Senior Common Room at Melhurst was the largest room in the whole school. It was frequented mainly by the Fifth, but the Sixth were not above using it for meeting and conversation, and at about teatime the room was usually packed. Prefects hardly used it at all, preferring the privacy of their studies.

With Darrell, of course, and, perhaps, Curtis, it was different. Many in the Fifth still found it difficult not to regard Darrell as one of themselves, and when he did show up they made him very welcome.

Whilst Darrell and the others were talking in the quadrangle, Denbigh, in the Senior Common Room, was telling an audience drawn entirely from the Sixth, how he had shown his contempt for Darrell. He stood by the fireplace, his hands in his pockets, recounting the incident to those around him.

" ' Denbigh ! ' he called out," said Denbigh, obviously enjoying himself. " ' I say, Denbigh ! ' Well, I just turned, looked at him, and then walked on."

" You didn't, really," said Richmond.

" I did. Hang it, haven't we said that we're going to cut the man ? Well, I did cut him."

" Of all the fools I've ever met, Denbigh, you're the biggest," said Wright, without looking up from the letter he was writing. " How you can swallow that rot about Darrell I don't know."

" Of course," sneered Denbigh, " it's only to be expected that the Fifth should stick up for their beloved Darrell. Even though he's been moved up you're still as thick as thieves. By Jove ! That's rather good—thick as thieves ! D'you see ? "

" More rot," said Wright, unmoved. " You and a lot more of the Sixth want to believe anything you hear against Darrell. You're all sore because he was made a prefect over you. And you don't like being routed out of bed for fielding practice either. Oh yes, we've heard all about that."

"I don't know what you're drivelling about," said Denbigh. "What's early morning fielding got to do with Darrell being a thief?"

"Probably quite a lot," said Mellish. "If he'd been very humble to you all you'd never have thought of helping to spread this story about him."

"Who's talking rot now?" inquired Bennet, though rather uncomfortably.

"It's not rot. A blind cart horse would know Darrell to be the very last person to have taken that money."

"Well, who else could have taken it?"

"What about you?"

"Me?"

"Yes, you. How do we know that you didn't break out of your dorm and pinch it?"

"Oh, for heaven's sake be sensible, man," said Denbigh impatiently. "Darrell's the only person who could have taken the money. Darrell's the thief, that's obvious."

" Would you say that to Darrell's face ? " asked Mellish.

" Yes, I would. Thieving's a thing I bar."

" I wonder if you'd have the pluck."

" Pluck ? Why, my dear man, didn't I just cut him in the quadrangle ? "

" That's different from calling him a thief to his face."

" Well, if he asks me to explain why I cut him, I shall tell him, that's all."

" That's very good of you, Denbigh," said a voice from the doorway. " What about telling me now ? "

A gasp rose from the occupants of the room as Darrell and his companions moved forward. Denbigh looked startled, and ran his finger round the inside of his collar. Then he waited, motionless, while Darrell came toward him.

" Well," said Darrell, " come on ! Here's your chance. Explain."

" If you heard what we were talking about I don't see that there's any need."

" Still, I'd rather hear it to my face."

" Very well, then, hear it to your face. I

think, as do most chaps, that you took that
money. We think you're the thief."

" And hasn't it struck you what a lot of fools
you are to think that ? "

" Why should it ? "

" Because, you infernal idiot, you haven't
got one atom of proof that I did it."

" No proof is needed. It's obvious."

" How is it ? Have I ever been suspected
of thieving before ? "

" Not that I know of."

" Then why should you think that I'm the
thief in this case ? "

" Because there's nothing else for us to
think."

" Agh ! " growled Darrell. " It's no good
arguing with you. You and your cronies want
to believe I'm a thief, and nothing's going to
stop you, is it ? Well, you can believe what
you like. You won't get many chaps to agree
with such a pack of idiots as you are."

" Do you think that we're the only ones who
believe it ? " said O'Neill. " Why, there are
lots of others."

" Yes, and how did it get about in the first place ? " put in Curtis.

" Well, things do get about, don't they ? "

" Not like this, unless they're deliberately spread by some one. Some one with a grudge against Darrell has made this up about him. A rumour's got to be started somewhere."

" How can any one work up a rumour without being found out ? " asked Kenton sceptically.

" Quite easily. Supposing *I* wanted to do it. I'd get hold of fellows separately and say something like this, ' Look here, do you believe this gossip about Darrell ? The fellows are saying *he* stole the money from his own cash-box. What do you think ? ' You see, I should be spreading a dirty lie without any one's realizing it."

" That's rather too far-fetched for yours truly," said Richmond.

" It would be," chimed in Collinson. " But it doesn't seem too far-fetched that Darrell should be a thief. Oh no ! "

" No, it doesn't," said O'Neill. " In fact, it seems very feasible."

" Say that again," said Larkin, stepping forward.

" Look here——" began Denbigh.

" Oh, it's all right," said Darrell, as Denbigh and those around him assumed defensive attitudes. " We're not going to slam you, or anything like that. I only wanted to find out how far this trick had gone. Come on, Larkin ; come on, you fellows, let's go down to field."

" Anyway——" said Collinson.

" Come on, don't let's waste any more time here."

They made a scornful exit from the room.

" It seems to me," said Mellish to Denbigh, " that you got rather squashed there."

Denbigh had at least been frank, but there were others who, believing Darrell to be guilty, gave him no chance to challenge them fairly. They were short with him in conversation, they exchanged meaning glances in his presence, but they avoided open accusation, and Darrell raged inwardly whilst keeping an outward composure.

For a time this form of conduct was confined

to the seniors, but before long it spread to the lower part of the school. While walking out of assembly one morning he distinctly heard the word "thief" spoken behind him. He turned sharply, but so great was the crowd around him that he could not hope to identify the speaker. This incident surprised Darrell, coming after a house match in which the juniors had cheered him for knocking up a century. It opened his eyes to the fickleness of crowds ; but he did not allow it to depress him for long.

As time went on Darrell concluded that Curtis was right in supposing the rumour to have been started and maintained of set purpose.

Among those who flatly refused to believe the accusation to be true was Anstruther, vice-captain of cricket, and Anstruther finally came over from Segal's to hear Darrell's own point of view.

"The Ferndale match is looming up," he said, as he sat down in Darrell's study. "Making any particular preparations ?"

"Early morning fielding for one," said Darrell.

"H'm!" said Anstruther thoughtfully. "I wonder what they'll say to it."

"I can't help what they say."

"Yes, but——"

"You mean," said Darrell, helping him out, "you wonder what they'll say about obeying the whim of a thief."

"Look here," said Anstruther frankly, "I want to tell you that I don't believe a word of it. In my opinion it's a lot of silly rot, and the fellows who talk about it are a lot of blithering idiots."

"Thanks. It's good to know that."

"How it got about in the first place *I* don't know."

"Somebody has set himself to keep the tale going. I am now regarded askance by most people, from prefects down to fags."

"Are you sure you aren't imagining a lot of this?"

"Imagining it? Listen!"

And Darrell recounted incidents of the past few days.

"Pretty rotten," said Anstruther. "I can still hardly believe it's all intentional."

" You can't easily imagine the things I've told you about. Look here, come down to the field with me now for some practice and you'll see what I mean."

" Right-o ! "

They reached the field without attracting more than a cursory attention. But nearing the First Eleven net, Darrell spun round, saying to Anstruther, " There, did you hear that ? "

He had just heard the word " thief," not on one boy's lips but on those of three or four. And this time he was able to place the culprits. They were juniors, almost old enough for the middle school, now standing with eyes studiously averted. He rapped out their names, " Lincoln, Gay, Avery, Hopgood, and Richardson, come here ! "

Play at the near-by Third and Second Eleven nets stopped dead. A crowd gathered round to see how Darrell would deal with the situation.

Darrell was really angry.

" Gay," he said, " go to my study and fetch me my cane. You'll find it in the cupboard."

" What for ? " demanded Gay, his face a veritable picture of injured innocence.

" You know very well what for," snapped Darrell. " I object to being called a thief."

" But hang it, Darrell ! " said Lincoln.

" Are you going, Gay ? " said Darrell quietly. " The longer you are about it, the harder it'll go with you."

Reluctantly Gay went. All five juniors were now feeling sorry for themselves. None of them had expected Darrell to use his authority like this.

Gay returned, and Darrell gave him and his four companions five strokes each. As he did so Darrell decided that there was more satisfaction in being a prefect than he had at one time suspected.

Giving his cane to Gay to take back, Darrell moved on with Anstruther to the First Eleven net. And the crowd, enlivened and impressed by the interlude, proceeded with their practice.

CHAPTER XIII

FIRST ELEVEN—REVISED

NEXT day, at " break," as the Sixth Form streamed from their classroom toward biscuits and milk in the dining-hall, they were interested by a notice on the school notice board. It ran as follows :

In view of the approaching Ferndale match the First Eleven will be required for a few early morning fielding practices. The first of these will take place to-morrow, beginning at 6.30 a.m., sharp.

R. S. DARRELL.

" Well, I'm jiggered," exploded Denbigh.

" Him ! " said Richmond ungrammatically, but with a wealth of meaning.

" Look here, Goulding," said Denbigh, " are

156

you going to stand for this ? Because I'm not."

" It is a bit thick," commented Goulding.

" Thick ? Why, it's colossal, frightful nerve."

" Well, I know what I am going to do," said Denbigh.

" What ? "

" I shan't be there."

"You mean you'll cut practice ? " said Kenton.

" You can bet. If you think I'm going to be routed out of bed an hour earlier by a thief, you're jolly well mistaken."

" All right, then, count me in too," said Richmond.

" And me," said Kenton.

" And me," echoed Bennet.

"What about you, Goulding ? " said Denbigh. Goulding thought for a moment, and said, " Look here ; I tell you what we'd better do first. You First Eleven chaps come along to my study after morning school."

" We're not all here, though," said Richmond, looking round him. " Anstruther and Alfriston are in the dining-hall."

" It doesn't matter about them," said Kenton. " They're pro-Darrell, in any case."

" That's so," agreed Goulding. " Just the eight of us ; that's all."

At five past twelve the eight had reassembled in Goulding's study.

" The thing to decide first," began Goulding, " is whether we can safely take it for granted that Darrell *was* the thief in that cash-box affair. No need for me to go into the details here, the Head did that in hall. We will simply put the matter to the vote. Those who think Darrel is guilty kindly raise a hand."

Eight hands were raised.

" Very good," said Goulding, " that's point Number One cleared up. Now we come to point Number Two. Darrell has informed us that he wants us out for early morning fielding practice. We don't think this is necessary, and we don't like taking orders from a thief. I suggest we send a note to Darrell demanding that he resign the cricket captaincy. If he refuses, then the eight of us resign our places in the Eleven."

There were murmurs of assent, swelling to an approving chorus.

" A thundering good idea ! " said Denbigh. " We hold him in the hollow of our hands."

" Do we ? " said Holmes uneasily.

" Well, what can he do besides resign ? "

" We aren't the only cricketers in the school, are we ? "

" Still, he wouldn't be such a priceless fool as to fill up our places with Second men."

" Even Darrell would hardly do that," said Goulding. " Now, I'll draft a note."

In a moment or two he read out the following ultimatum :

" ' DEAR DARRELL,—In view of recent events we, the undersigned, think that you will best serve the interests of Melhurst by resigning the cricket captaincy. If you do not agree to do so we request that you accept our immediate resignations from the First Eleven.' "

" How's that ? " he inquired.

His followers made sounds indicating their approval.

"I'll sign first," said Goulding, "then you others, in any order. And I'll get a fag to take it along."

He went to the window and called out to a fag named Rawson in the quadrangle below.

When the fag appeared Goulding gave him the note, told him to take it to whom it was addressed, and wait for an answer.

With the air of one who bears important tidings the fag trotted along to Darrell's study. Darrell was at home in company with Larkin, Collinson, and Curtis. He read the note, laughed shortly, and told Rawson to wait outside. Then he handed the note to the others.

"I might have expected it," he said.

"But, good lord," said Collinson blankly, "they don't mean it, do they?"

"Of course they mean it."

"But you're not going to resign, are you?"

"Resign? If I did I'd be properly branded as a thief. Every one would think it an admission of guilt on my part. No, not on your life!"

"What are you going to do, then?"

" Accept their resignations, of course."

" But how is the First going to get on ? " asked Larkin in amazement.

" From now on you can consider yourself a member," said Darrell. " And Collinson. I'll fill the vacant places with Second men."

" But the Ferndale match comes off next week."

" I couldn't help it if we were playing Surrey. You're not funking, are you ? "

" Lord, no ! "

" Golly ! " said Collinson, his eyes gleaming. " What a go ! But, dash it ! it's the only thing you can do. You'd be a fool to kowtow to them. That's just what they want."

" And it's just what they're not going to get. Here, Rawson, come in ! Take this back to Goulding, will you ? "

He scribbled a few lines on a piece of paper torn from his notebook and gave it to Rawson, who bore it carefully back to Goulding with the same air of importance. Goulding took the note and began to read it with the carelessness of one to whom the contents were a foregone conclusion. But as he read his expression changed.

" Good heavens, he's actually done it ! " he gasped.

" What ? " said Denbigh.

" Accepted our resignations."

" What rot ! "

" See for yourself."

" Well, I'm hanged ! " said Denbigh. " The fool ! How's the First going to get on without us ? "

" What does Darrell care about the First ? " said Goulding savagely. " It's himself that he looks after. Nobody else or anything matters besides."

" We shall get properly tanned by Ferndale," said Kenton.

" I had a sort of feeling that's what he'd do," said Holmes gloomily.

" Who cares ? " said Denbigh.

But it was obvious that he did care, that they all cared very much indeed. And as Denbigh and the rest took their leave of Goulding more than one of them looked resentfully at him.

After dinner Darrell posted up a list of the members of the reconstructed First Eleven. The news spread quickly, and the notice board was besieged by an excited mob.

And when the new Eleven went to the nets for their first practice, practically the whole school turned up as spectators. Absorbed, they watched the play of the new-comers—the wicket-keeping of Jakes, the slow bowling of Mellish, and the batting of Osborne, Wright, and Collinson. On the whole, they came through their ordeal with credit, and later, in fielding practice, their form was at least as good as that of their predecessors. Taking everything into account, Darrell did not despair of their chance of losing only by a small margin, or even of forcing a draw.

CHAPTER XIV

MELHURST *VERSUS* FERNDALE

THE day of the Ferndale match was brilliantly fine. It was, of course, a whole holiday, and hot sunlight combined with the excitement to make of it a most memorable occasion.

At half-past ten the Ferndale team turned up in a motor coach. Darrell waited at the gates to meet them. He knew Gascoyne, the Ferndale captain, having played against him in previous years.

Gascoyne, who was tall and slight, walked with a gentle sway and wore a small moustache, parted neatly in the middle. His brushed-back hair shone with brilliantine, his voice was high and inane, and he made great play with a scented silk handkerchief. But to Darrell, who had seen him hit up a century off good bowling, his appearance and affectations made no difference.

" I think you're going to get a licking to-day," said Darrell when they met outside the pavilion for the toss.

" Here goes," he added, and spun a coin in the air.

" Heads ! " called out Gascoyne ; and heads it was.

" I think we'll bat," said Gascoyne.

" Right," said Darrell.

The crowd round the ropes was almost silent as Melhurst took the field. The Fifth Form raised a lonely cheer, and a few of the masters clapped, but the bulk of the school reserved their applause for Gascoyne and Blaize, the Ferndale opening batsmen.

" Middle and leg," called out Blaize to the umpire from the batting end.

The umpire spoke a few throaty words, Blaize moved his bat accordingly, the fieldsmen assumed their correct positions, Anstruther measured out ten paces and threw his cap on the ground to mark the beginning of his run. Blaize looked round, patted the turf in front of his crease, and stood on guard ; for a moment every one was still, dead white against the green of the grass and the blue of the hot summer sky. Then Anstruther began his run, and the match was on its way.

Anstruther's first ball was perfect. It swerved in from the off at breath-taking speed, in direct line for the leg stump. Blaize banged his bat down and managed to stop it dead. Then he whistled softly to himself and looked at Anstruther with respect.

The first over was a maiden. As Mellish took the ball at the other end, Darrell settled himself at cover with anxiety in his heart. Mellish was taking Richmond's place as slow bowler ; he had already deputized for him once before during the season, but on that occasion had only come up against the tail of the opposing team.

Mellish took a short run and bowled. The ball was meant to break in from the leg. But Gascoyne did not allow it to break, or even to bounce. He jumped out of his crease like a panther and hit the ball over mid-on's head for six. The next ball he let alone, the third he hit for two, the fifth he blocked, and the sixth he swept round past square-leg for four. Altogether, it was an expensive over for the home team.

" Dashed sorry, Darrell," said Mellish as they crossed over. " You'd better take me off."

" Lord, no ! Not yet. You'll probably do better next over."

" I dunno what it was, but I couldn't get my length."

" It was Gascoyne. Look out for him. He hits bad-length balls and good-length ones as well. He never seems to bother to play himself in. Don't let him frighten you."

The last ball of the next over went for two, and Mellish had again to bowl against Gascoyne. The first ball was a good one, and Gascoyne, playing forward, lifted it a little. When Collinson threw the ball back to Mellish, the latter motioned him farther in. Collinson nodded, and took up a position a few steps nearer the batsman, his eyes puckered up, for he was facing the sun. Mellish ran . . . the ball sped on its way . . . Gascoyne jumped out with upraised bat and hit . . . Collinson flung up his hand, and the ball brushed it and struck him over one eye. He sank to the ground with both hands to his head.

Gascoyne rushed to pick him up, and a knot of figures gathered round.

" Darned sorry," said Gascoyne.

Collinson's face was puckered up with pain. On his forehead was an angry red mark, swelling rapidly into a purple bruise.

" How d'you feel ? " asked Darrell anxiously. " Pretty bad ? Here, Larkin, help me get him to the pavilion."

Larkin came forward, and between them they half carried Collinson to the pavilion. Luckily Dr. Hilary, the school doctor, was watching the match, and taking charge of Collinson, he led him gently away.

Ackroyd, who was ready as substitute, came up to Darrell.

" You'll want me to field ? " he said.

Darrell nodded, and strode disconsolately back to the pitch. He had depended on Collinson as a bat, and this misfortune seemed a scurvy trick of Fate.

But if the accident to Collinson dismayed Darrell, it upset Gascoyne. Staunch cricketer and fop though he was, Gascoyne hated the sight of any one getting hurt. He hit at Mellish's next ball without his usual timed skill. The ball broke, scraped his bat, and Alfriston at first slip flung himself forward and caught it before he fell.

Most of the spectators had watched the beginning of the game with some degree of hostility towards Darrell and his side. The accident to Collinson considerably modified this feeling. Whatever might be said about Darrell, it was bad luck that he should be deprived of an important member of his side when the game had hardly started. And now Ferndale's crack batsman had been dismissed for a paltry nineteen.

The Melhurst crowd broke into vociferous applause. The next man in, a short, stocky individual, marched to the wicket with all the confidence of a professional cricketer. Mellish took an instant dislike to him. It may have been owing to this dislike, or to the fact that Mellish had suddenly found his length, but the fact remained that next moment the stocky batsman was gazing at Jakes, the wicket-keeper, who was engaged in setting the middle stump back into its proper position.

" Well, I'm hanged ! " he ejaculated. " Surely that didn't bowl me ? "

" The middle stump's been knocked over, anyhow," said Jakes.

With a dark look on his face, as if he suspected foul play, the batsman strutted off the field again.

The spirits of the Melhurst team rose with a bound. Two for nineteen was something like a catastrophe for their opponents. Nevertheless the Ferndale teams were famous for their lack of a tail.

The third man in was of an impassive type. From the start of his innings he played the bowling with quiet but masterly confidence. Blaize and he settled down to a partnership. From thirty the score mounted to fifty, and then to eighty. Blaize was hitting out in all directions, whilst his partner added ones and twos.

When the hundred was up and the fieldsmen were crossing at the end of the over, Anstruther said to Darrell :

" I say, what about trying me on at the other end ? I have a hunch I'd have more luck there."

" All right," said Darrell. " I'll put Ralston on for an over at this end. And I think I'll give Mellish a rest."

Anstruther's first ball from the other end Blaize's partner hit for two, and the next for four. But the third had him beaten. It was a yorker, and knocked his off-stump clean into the wicket-keeper's hands. And with his dismissal the game was adjourned for lunch.

As soon as he had reached the pavilion Darrell inquired after Collinson.

" Oh, he's getting on all right," said the doctor. " I've left him taking it easy in his study."

" Will he be able to bat ? "

The doctor shook his head.

" I don't think so. His head's bandaged, and it must be painful."

Darrell smiled wryly.

"We were depending on him, too. Substitutes aren't allowed to do anything more than field, of course. Still, we'll have to manage as best we can."

After lunch play was less eventful, Anstruther and Mellish bowling a number of maiden overs. Then runs began to mount up again. The hundred and thirty mark was reached, and at a hundred and thirty-six Blaize was caught in the outfield.

From then on wickets fell with some regularity, but not before most of the Ferndale batsmen had contributed their fair share of runs. The top score was Blaize's fifty-two, but the second lowest was fifteen. And when the Ferndale innings closed, the total stood at two hundred and forty-six. Such a score would take some getting against the Ferndale bowling, even by a strong team, let alone by a team in which eight places were filled by Second Eleven men.

CHAPTER XV

DARRELL WINS THROUGH

FERNDALE had taken the field, and Darrell and Alfriston went out to bat. The clapping, perfunctory at first, swelled as they neared the wicket. There was no cheering, for the crowd was at a loss as to how it should treat Darrell.

" Middle," said Darrell to the umpire.

The umpire informed him that he had middle, and Darrell, not usually superstitious, took that as an omen that he was to stay some time at the wicket. Round him the fieldsmen gathered, and before him Mercer, the Ferndale fast bowler, was marking out the spot where his run began. The crowd round the field now included the Head, his wife and family, and most of the staff, together with a few old gaffers from the village who were accorded the privilege of watching matches at Melhurst.

For a second or two Darrell's thoughts were far away. He was a small boy again, sitting with his father on the top of Beachy Head. In front of them glittered the sea, and on their left Eastbourne shimmered in the haze of afternoon. And his father was saying, "Yes, when the odds against one are greatest, then the struggle is the most glorious."

Well, two hundred and forty-six was a good score, especially when one took into account their own weakness ; but, hang it ! let them have a shot at it.

Mercer was running now. He came to the wicket, his arm swung round, and the ball hummed towards Darrell at speed. Darrell played it carefully. The second and third he blocked, but the fourth he hit hard past Gascoyne at mid-on for three. Alfriston contented himself with stonewalling the remaining balls of the over, and then Darrell faced the slow bowler.

The slow bowler was a tubby youth with a

shock of sandy hair. His action when bowling was perhaps the oddest that Darrell had ever seen. At the end of a short hopping run he seemed to trip as though he were going to fall, and then delivered the ball with an apparently awkward swing. Instinctively Darrell got ready to swipe, thinking, "This fellow looks hopeless."

As he jumped out of his crease a premonition assailed him ; darting back, he banged his bat down on the ball as it spun in from the off. Gascoyne looked at him as though to say, "Nearly had you there, didn't we ? "

Darrell grinned and breathed a sigh of relief.

Again came those curious hops, the slip that was almost a tumble, and the perfectly pitched ball whipping in from the off. But this time Darrell was ready for it. He played the ball past cover, and they ran a single. Alfriston, who benefited from Darrell's experience, treated this bowling with tremendous care. But the last ball of the over, a loose one, he swept round to leg for a two.

In the next over Darrell hit his first boundary. The ball came very fast on the off, and timing it perfectly, he cut it clean through the slips for four. A cheer rose from the crowd, and a flush mounted to Darrell's cheeks. Every moment the atmosphere was becoming less strained ; being temperamental when at the wicket, he responded noticeably to it. The next ball he hit for four, the third he hooked past square-leg for two, and the fifth he slammed clean into the pavilion for six. At this a loud burst of applause resounded. Some one shouted, " Well played, Darrell ! " and the cry was taken up and repeated all round the ground.

" Darrell seems to be very popular," said Mrs. Alcott to her husband.

The Head nodded.

" He does, doesn't he ? But then a boy of his type usually is."

His wife surveyed the field through her *lorgnette*.

" But surely these aren't the same boys who were playing last time ? " she said. " It seems to be quite a new eleven."

" Yes, there have been several changes. No doubt Darrell knows what he is doing."

The score went up by leaps and bounds. Fifty, a hundred, a hundred and fifty displaced each other on the scoring-board, with Darrell and Alfriston still impregnable. By teatime the former had made eighty-nine, and the latter sixty-four. Gascoyne had tried bowler after bowler, all to no purpose.

" You're lost at Melhurst," said Gascoyne to Darrell as they made their way to the pavilion for the fifteen minutes' tea interval. " You ought to have come to Ferndale."

" Ferndale ? Good lord ! " grinned Darrell.

" You haven't won yet," Gascoyne told him. " Not by a long chalk. Once we get you two out we'll mow the rest of your side like corn."

" You'll find them pretty tough corn. We're thinking of taking on Surrey and a few other county teams."

Gascoyne raised his eyebrows in astonishment.

" My dear man ! D'you mean to say that you haven't played any county teams yet ? Why, we meet 'em regularly. The matches aren't reported, of course, because it looks bad when county teams are licked by a school."

" As a matter of fact," said Darrell solemnly, " we haven't taken on any county teams yet because we've rather thought ourselves above it. But they've begged us so often to give them a game that we're thinking of changing our minds. Believe it or not."

" Oh, I believe you," said Gascoyne.

" So do I," said a voice.

They turned to find Collinson on the pavilion steps.

" Collinson, by Jove ! " said Darrell. " How are you feeling ? "

" Oh, all right. A bit wonky, but that's all."

" I'm awfully sorry about it, y'know, old bean," said Gascoyne earnestly. " I am, really."

" Oh, that's all right. You didn't know I was going to get in the way, did you ? "

" By gad, I didn't ! Much of a bruise under that bandage ? "

" Pretty big. I've really come down here against the doctor's orders. I said I'd play even if I hadn't a head to play with. But it turns out there's no need. You're actually going to get licked, Gascoyne."

"You wait. There's still another couple of hours' play."

During tea Darrell found himself the centre of attraction. Juniors edged up to him and listened to every word he uttered with a respectful silence. Middle and senior schoolboys tried to get into conversation with him.

"I may be a thief," thought Darrell, "but they're willing to forget that for my cricket."

And he didn't know whether to be pleased or annoyed.

At half-past five the white figures reassembled on the wide expanse of green, and Mercer, sent back to the attack by Gascoyne after a rest, commenced his old familiar run. The ball whizzed wickedly from his hand, and Alfriston, playing forward, missed it. The ball struck his pad.

"S'that?" inquired Mercer and several others.

The umpire put up his finger, and Alfriston trotted back towards the pavilion. A burst of cheering greeted him. He had made a chance-less sixty-four off very good bowling.

Wright came to the wicket as the cheering subsided, and by the jerky way in which he took guard, Darrell could tell that he was nervous. Darrell smiled encouragingly, and Wright grinned back. Then he prepared himself for the first ball. It came, and shattered his wicket.

And then a rot set in. Batsman succeeded batsman at intervals of less than ten minutes. One for a hundred and fifty-three, three for a hundred and sixty, five for a hundred and seventy-five, seven for a hundred and eighty. Darrell passed his century amid cheers, but there was a strained note in them.

Darrell was now playing like one possessed. He seized every chance of scoring, and every chance of securing the bowling. Anstruther stayed with him for half an hour to make fourteen, but then was hopelessly beaten by a ball from Mercer.

The score stood at two hundred and five for eight. There was only one more man to come in, unless Collinson came out to bat. But could the damaged Collinson face that fast bowler ? If so, there was still a chance that the game could be pulled out of the fire.

Mellish, the ninth man in, stayed for three overs, during which time the Ferndale side stood on their toes for the slightest chance that might be offered them. Then Mellish was yorked by Mercer, and the players gazed inquiringly towards the pavilion.

" Is Collinson able to bat, Darrell ? " asked Gascoyne. " Because, if not . . ."

A cheer went round the field, for Collinson had emerged from the pavilion, his hands busy with his gloves, and his head encased in a large panama hat.

" Oh, here he is," said Gascoyne. " Good man ! Clap, you fellows."

And the Ferndale team added their applause to the rest.

Mellish's wicket had fallen to the first ball of the over, and so Collinson, unless he succeeded in changing places with Darrell, had five balls to come. The first ball from Mercer he stopped dead. To Darrell's pleasure he did not scratch awkwardly at it, but played it confidently with the centre of his bat. And the next he jumped out at and smote to the boundary. Darrell could have danced with delight.

The pair settled down, Collinson playing quietly but confidently, and Darrell hitting out all round the wicket. And the hands of the clock moved steadily on towards half-past seven, when stumps would be drawn whatever the state of the game.

The crowd had grown silent. The only sounds to be heard were the " chock " of bat meeting ball, the shout of one fielder to another, the batsman's urgent word to his partner as they started another run. With ten minutes still to go, Melhurst needed fourteen for a win. Could they possibly do it ?

Slowly but steadily the hands of the clock moved on. Twenty-two, twenty-four, twenty-five minutes past . . . and the white figures ran and the crowd became still with the fixity of graven images.

" Last over ! " called one of the umpires, his voice ringing out in the hush.

The last over, and ten to win. Darrell had the bowling and the slow bowler. The second ball he hit for three, and then it was Collinson's turn. The third ball Collinson managed to force past cover for a single, and Darrell was back at the batting end again.

Six to win and three balls to come. . . . The fourth ball Darrell hooked past square leg for two, the fifth he hit hard in the direction of Gascoyne at mid-on ; but the tall Ferndale captain dived sideways, stopped it, and threw it back to the wicket-keeper as he fell. Darrell regained his crease just in time.

Last ball. . . .

The bowler took his run, and the ball had hardly left his hand when Darrell swept out of his crease for one of the mightiest hits ever seen on the Melhurst ground. The ball soared, seemed to hover as a black speck in the velvety blue, and then hurtled down to drop behind the pavilion.

With that all restraint left the crowd, and,

climbing over the ropes, they made straight for the players.

" Darrell ! " they roared. " Darrell ! "

" I say," said Gascoyne, " you'd better run if you don't want to get mobbed."

Darrell ran.

He had made one hundred and thirty-two not out.

Chapter XVI

SIMS COMES TO TEA

DARRELL the "thief" was forgotten, and
Darrell the cricketer reigned in his stead.
It was more or less generally agreed that some
queer mistake had been made. Darrell had not
looked forward with pleasure to making a
second collection for the end-of-term cricket
spread, but almost every one was alert to show
him how public opinion had changed.

Nevertheless, Darrell was not altogether
happy. His name was not yet cleared ; the
identity of the real thief remained a complete
mystery. Inquiries set on foot by the Head
had borne no fruit, and had eventually been
dropped.

And so, for the time at any rate, the matter
rested in abeyance—until Sims, last year's

captain of cricket, elected to visit his old school.

Entering his study one day about five o'clock, with Larkin, Collinson, and Curtis close behind him, Darrell found, to his surprise, a figure seated in a chair, holding in one hand a glass of ginger beer, and in the other a plate of bread and butter.

" Well, of all the cheek——" began Darrell.

" Make yourselves at home," said the intruder affably. " Don't mind me."

" You can——" And then Darrell stopped, stared, and burst into a howl of laughter. " Sims ! " he sobbed. " Is it you ? My hat ! "

His three companions gazed inquiringly at the object of his mirth, and then joined in the laughter. For the rubicund countenance of Sims was adorned by a small moustache and imperial.

" When you've finished," said Sims in a pained voice.

" But what on earth's made you grow the thing ? " asked Darrell, wiping his eyes.

" I belong to a club at St. Jude's. It's called

the Imperial Club. It consists of about twenty fellows, and we all wear moustaches and imperials."

" You must look a rum lot when you meet. Well, don't let any of the fellows here catch you, that's all."

" Why not ? "

" Because they'll shave the things off."

" They wouldn't."

" They would. Don't you remember when old Carsbole turned up, after leaving, with a beard, and how they yanked him into the Senior Common Room and burnt part of it off before shaving the rest ? "

" Good lord ! " exclaimed Sims, fingering his moustache. " I must be careful. I'm going to visit the Head after tea. I'd better go by a roundabout way."

" You bet you had. Well, how do you like Cambridge ? "

The question gave Sims plenty to talk about. To Darrell's relief the conversation did not touch on school cricket, for one or two embarrassing points might have been raised.

At half-past five Sims got up to go and pay his respects to the Head.

" Has term finished at Cambridge ? " asked Darrell.

" Yes. A week ago."

" Good heavens, what a time you must have. You're not staying at the school, are you ? "

" No, I'm putting up at the ' Peal o' Bells ' in the village for a couple of nights. Billiards every night till twelve. And—that reminds me, I've got something to tell you that might interest you. I was in the billiard-room there last night when a fellow from the school came in. He was in the Fifth when I left, but I expect he's in the Sixth now. I had a shock when I saw him, I can tell you, but not such a shock as he had."

" But what was he doing there ? " asked Larkin.

" He'd broken out of school to play billiards, of course. And the landlord told me—this is just between ourselves, don't forget—that the chap owes him quite a lot of money."

" What's his name ? " asked Darrell.

" Um, let me think now." Sims thought, and then shook his head. " No, I can't tell you for the life of me. Whoever he is, he must be pretty flush, because he owed the landlord close on twelve pounds over billiards not long ago, and paid him off at one shot."

" Twelve pounds ? " said Darrell, staring.

" Yes."

" Look here," said Darrell excitedly. " Do try to remember this fellow's name. It might prove important."

" How ? Well, don't let it out, will you ? I don't want to get him into a row."

Again he thought, hard this time, but again he shook his head.

" I'm hanged if I can tell you."

" What's he like ? "

" Oh, you know him. He—here, I'll tell you something. His name reminded me of a county in England. Hang it, why can't I think of it ? "

" Not Denbigh," said Curtis.

" No. Besides, that's in Wales."

" Stafford ? " asked Collinson.

" No."

" Cornwallis ? " asked Larkin.

" No." And then Sims flicked his fingers with satisfaction. " Ah, I've got it. Kenton."

" Kenton," repeated Darrell, Larkin, Collinson, and Curtis together.

" Yes, Kenton," said Sims, as he moved to the door. " He's run up another debt of eight pounds as it is. The landlord made me laugh. D'you know how he got the other money ? "

" No."

" All in sixpences. Funny, wasn't it ? So long."

" Kenton ! " said Darrell again, when Sims had gone. " So he's the slug who pinched the money ? "

" Why on earth didn't we think of him before ? " said Curtis. " *He* must have put that rumour about. He's the one fellow in the school with real cause for a grudge against Darrell."

" How ? " asked Collinson.

" Why, wasn't Darrell made a prefect in place of him ? "

" And that night when we broke out to dress

up old Cody's statue," said Larkin eagerly, " Kenton was the chap whom I chased and who locked us out. He must have been returning from a jaunt at the ' Peal o' Bells.' "

" Jove ! " said Darrell. " It all fits in like the pieces in a jig-saw puzzle."

" The swine ! " from Larkin.

" The hound ! " from Collinson.

Darrell got up with a look of determination on his face.

" Come on," he said.

" Where ? " inquired Curtis.

" To Kenton's study, of course. Tax him with the theft of the money, make him confess to it, and haul him before the Head ! "

" Wait a minute, though," said Curtis.

" But——"

" Wait a minute. Suppose he denies it all, what are you going to do ? It's only Sims's word against his."

" There's the landlord of the ' Peal o' Bells.' We can ask him how Kenton paid him back the money he owed him."

" And if he thinks there's going to be any

trouble about it, he'll deny that Kenton has ever as much as set foot in his place."

" Well," said Darrell blankly, " what are we going to do ? "

" Anything rather than rush in bald-headed and muck everything up."

" What do you suggest, then ? "

" Let me think."

There was a silence. Curtis got up and began to pace about the room, hands in his pockets, gaze fixed on the floor. Darrell stood staring meditatively out of the window. Larkin propped himself thoughtfully up against the mantelpiece. Collinson sat chewing a jam tart very slowly, as though he did not even know that he was eating.

Then, suddenly, Curtis stopped his perambulations and seated himself at the table.

" I think I've got it," he said. " The thing to do is to set a trap for Kenton. Think out some scheme whereby he gives away the whole bally bag of tricks, so that Darrell's name is cleared for good and all. Now, Sims told us that Kenton owes the landlord of the ' Peal o'

Bells' another eight pounds. Almost certainly he's hard pressed to find the money. That's one thing to remember. And the other is that the window in the prefects' room hasn't been mended yet."

"The porters are so beastly slack," said Darrell. "I don't suppose it'll get mended till the holidays."

"Well, listen," said Curtis, and unfolded his plan.

"But do you think that Kenton 'll allow himself to be trapped so easily?" asked Darrell, when he had finished.

"He may not. But it's worth trying. We shan't be any the worse if he doesn't, shall we?"

"Rather not. Now, first of all we'll need a fag to give instructions to. Rutley 'll do. Give him a shilling and he'll do anything you want."

Rutley was summoned, and, to his gratification, found himself in earnest confabulation with the captain of cricket, another prefect, and two of the famous eight promoted members of the Second Eleven.

CHAPTER XVII

THE SMALL HOURS AGAIN

KENTON sat alone in his study, staring before him with unseeing eyes. He owed the landlord of the "Peal o' Bells" eight pounds; he had not, and was not likely to have, eight pounds to pay him with. The landlord was pressing for settlement of this debt, and had even threatened that he might report the matter to the headmaster. Possibly this was bluff, thought Kenton, but again, possibly not. Last time he managed nicely—and what a fool he had been to get into the same mess again.

His meditations were cut short by the appearance of the diminutive Rutley.

" Please, Kenton, Goulding wants to see you in the prefects' room," he said.

" What for ? "

" I don't know."

" All right, you can go."

Stretching himself, Kenton followed Rutley out of the room, and, descending into the quadrangle, hurried across to the prefects' room in the school buildings. When he opened the door, however, he found that Goulding was not there. The only occupants of the room were Darrell and Curtis. Both were seated at Darrell's table ; Darrell had his cash-box open, and was engaged in counting the heaps of sixpences. For some time Kenton watched him, forgetful of the reason of his presence in the room, until Curtis looked round.

" Well ? " he said.

" Goulding wanted to see me here," said Kenton.

" Oh, he's just gone out. He'll be back shortly. You'd better wait. Take a chair."

Kenton sat down and watched the other two and the gleaming piles of money in silence.

" Well, that's right," said Darrell, with a sigh of relief. " Twelve pounds, fourteen and six. The same as last time."

"When does the Head want it?" asked Curtis.

"To-morrow."

"This time, I expect, you'll take the cash-box to bed with you and sleep on it."

"Oh no. I shall leave it here as usual."

"What, with the window still broken?" asked Curtis, in apparent amazement.

"Yes. It can't possibly be rifled a second time."

"I'm not so jolly well sure."

"Oh, I am. It'll be all right."

"Well, if you find the money gone to-morrow, my boy, don't say I didn't warn you. And this time the Head would regard you with a fishy eye. As for the fellows . . ."

"It'll be all right, I tell you," said Darrell. "Here, I'll leave it on this table. Coming back to house?"

"Yes."

As Darrell opened the door, Rutley again materialized and presented himself before Kenton.

"Oh, Kenton," he said, "Goulding said it doesn't matter after all."

" Well, I'm blest. What on earth's the matter with the man ? Is he crazy ? "

With a propitiatory smile on his face Rutley sidled away. Kenton returned slowly to his house, so deep in thought that he reached his study and sat down without knowing it. . . . Eight pounds . . . twelve pounds, fourteen and six. . . .

And in Darrell's study Collinson said :

" Well, how did it work ? "

" All right, I think," said Darrell. " He seemed to be watching us pretty intently, didn't he, Curtis ? "

" Dunno. There wasn't anything or any one else to watch really, was there ? "

" Still, let's hope for the best. If he doesn't try and break out of the house to-night to steal that money a second time, then I'm a Dutchman."

" I say ! " said Larkin suddenly. " Supposing he meets Goulding before bed to-night, and asks Goulding what he was supposed to have wanted him for. Goulding 'll tell him that he knows nothing about it, and Kenton will smell a rat. Why on earth didn't we think of that before ? "

" You needn't worry," Curtis told him. " That eventuality hadn't escaped me. As a matter of fact Goulding is visiting an aunt of his, who lives not far from the village, at this moment. I'm the only fellow who knows about it. We were in his study together, just before I came to tea with you, when he got a telegram asking him to come quickly and pay his dutiful respects to her, as she's suddenly decided to go away for some time. He went there and then, asking me to tell any one all about it who wanted to know where he was. I had that in mind all along. I ought to have told you."

" Well, then, what about to-night ? " said Collinson.

" That's the next thing to think about," agreed Darrell. " Let's see, now. We don't want to run into Kenton on our way to the prefects' room."

" Rather not."

" What about meeting on the front corridor

of the first floor—you know, the same spot as before—at half-past eleven, then ? "

" That'll be the best time," said Curtis. " There'll be no moon to-night, thank the lord."

" The fates are with us," said Collinson.

" I wouldn't mind betting," remarked Darrell, " that Kenton is thinking the same thing."

Darrell lay on his bed, half dressed, staring into the darkness. As he came to bed later than the others he rarely put the dormitory lights on ; no one else in the room could tell that he had not undressed as usual.

The luminous dial of his watch showed that the time was five minutes to eleven. He had over half an hour to wait, and already he was so tired that he found it difficult not to close his eyes. He thought of cricket, of the holidays now not far ahead, of Kenton, of that blue-nosed baboon, the landlord of the " Peal o' Bells." Darrell had no sympathy for Kenton, and considered that the landlord ought to be shot. Darrell, Larkin, and Collinson themselves had once broken out of school at night on a visit to the " Peal o' Bells " and had lost three pounds at cards between them. All three were sure that the landlord had cheated, but they had no evidence of the fact. " Well, if that's night life," said Darrell in disgust, as they came away afterwards, " I don't want any more of it. We'll have to pawn the school plate to see us through the rest of the term."

Consciousness slowly receded from him, and he roused himself with a jerk.

Half-past eleven ! The time had arrived. Darrell got up, put on the few clothes he had taken off, took his shoes in hand, and crept out of his dormitory. When he reached the back landing of the first floor he found the others waiting for him.

Without a word Larkin opened the window and disappeared over the sill. Curtis, going next, was directed by Darrell from above and Larkin from below how best to negotiate the descent. Collinson followed, and Darrell went down last.

So dark was it that twice they had to halt

to get their bearings. Eventually they were brought up short by the ivy-covered wall of the school, and a few paces more brought them under the prefects' window.

Darrell climbed on to the sill and disappeared into the room, the others quickly following.

" You see how easy it is," whispered Darrell. " It was the simplest thing in the world for him to have taken that money."

" How shall we wait ? " asked Collinson. " Just sit about ? "

" No fear," said Curtis. " Probably he'd have a torch and he'd see us as soon as he was on the window-sill. We'd better get where we can't be seen."

" Three of us can sit on the floor behind those armchairs," said Darrell, " and another on a chair behind those curtains over there."

" That'll do nicely."

They took up their various positions and settled down to wait. They did not speak, the slightest sound might endanger the success of their design.

From his position behind the curtains Darrell

sat with his ears strained for signs of an intruder. For a long time he heard only the beating of his own heart, the faint ticking of the clock on the mantelpiece, and, now and then, the rustle of ivy outside the window.

From behind his chair Collinson yawned and endeavoured to compose himself more comfortably. Longingly he thought of his nice warm bed. How inviting it had looked when he had left it, and how uncomfortable his present position on the floor ! Not that the vigil wasn't worth while, of course, but bed always seemed particularly alluring when one was feeling cramped and cold.

From behind another chair Larkin polished his glasses with a handkerchief. They did not require polishing, nor did the process help him to see any more clearly in the dark, but it was better than just sitting and doing nothing. Then he took a piece of paper out of his pocket, and, using his knee as a rest, began tracing invisible patterns on it with a pencil.

Behind a third chair Curtis sat huddled, hands in his pockets and chin almost resting on his knees. He had forgotten the awkwardness of his position in recollecting a tricky passage from Balzac's *Pierrette*.

One . . . two . . . three . . . the school clock chimed twelve. Then there was silence again. Then the quarter, and silence. The half-hour, and silence. Collinson snored faintly, and gulped himself awake. The three-quarters rang out, and each of the four began to tell himself that this waiting was sheer stupidity.

One o'clock. Darrell stretched himself and sighed. Would Kenton never come ? Would they have to give up with his own name still uncleared ? Would . . . And then Darrell suddenly stiffened. His ears had caught a faint scraping outside the window. Then came a soft thud as some one mounted the window-sill. A beam of light shone in the room, swept uncertainly round the walls, and rested on Darrell's cash-box.

The circle of light brightened as it diminished. The money chinked and slithered as the box was moved.

Darrell rose silently from his chair, hardly

daring to breathe. His hand crept along the wall towards the electric switch, found the knob, and pressed it down.

The room was flooded with light, so strong after the dark that his eyes blinked. Darrell pushed the curtain aside, and Larkin, Collinson, and Curtis rose from their hiding-places.

The intruder had gasped and swung round.

" Kenton ! " exclaimed Collinson triumphantly.

" You're caught, my boy," growled Larkin.

" I told you we'd get him," claimed Curtis calmly.

" Now we know ! " said Darrell.

" What d'you mean ? " cried Kenton, his eyes starting out of his head, his body literally shaking with fright.

" What do we mean ! " scoffed Darrell. " Does that require any explanation ? " pointing to the cash-box already open on the table. " We heard how you got into debt at the ' Peal o' Bells,' and how you paid the landlord in sixpences, and so Curtis thought out a scheme to make you give yourself away. And now

Larkin hurled himself sideways and managed to grab Kenton just as
he reached the window-sill.

you're coming along with us to Mr. Sparrow. We're going to wake him up and make you explain everything."

" No," said Kenton violently.

" Oh yes, we are," said Collinson.

Kenton cast a hunted look round him, and made a dash for the window.

" By Jove, on him, some one ! " said Darrell.

Larkin hurled himself sideways and managed to grab Kenton just as he reached the window-sill. He brought him down to the floor with a bump, and the others jumped forward into the fray. Kenton fought with strength and ferocity almost as though for his life. His coat was torn off his back, his face was bruised, and his nose was bleeding before he began to weaken. With Darrell hanging on to his legs, Collinson sitting on his chest, and Larkin and Curtis each holding on to an arm, he finally subsided, powerless to move.

" It's no good, Kenton," said Darrell. " We've got you all right."

Kenton said nothing, but glared up at him with an almost insane fury.

" What shall we——"

But Collinson never finished what he began to say. A cold commanding voice interrupted him.

" What does this mean, may I ask ? "

The Head stood in the doorway of the room.

Darrell, Larkin, Collinson, and Curtis got to their feet, and allowed Kenton to do the same, not forgetting to keep a firm hold on him.

" Will some one explain ? " rasped the Head. " Working much later than usual in my study, I happened to look out of the window and saw a light shining in this room."

Then Darrell let go his grip of the prisoner and stepped forward to confront the Head. Beginning with Sims's momentous piece of information he proceeded to explain Curtis's plan, its execution, and the *dénouement*. As the sequence of events was unfolded, the Head's brow grew black as thunder. When Darrell had finished the Head turned to Kenton with a look on his face that frightened Darrell and his companions. The latter released their wretched captive, and the Head spoke again.

" Tell me the truth, Kenton," he said. " Did you take that money ? "

Kenton lifted an ashen face.

" I took it," he said huskily. " I don't deny it."

In quick, jerky sentences he made a fairly clean breast of the affair, only slurring over his attempt to lay the blame on Darrell's shoulders. It was a miserable story ; even Darrell and the others grew ashamed to listen.

" I meant to pay the money back," he concluded, as if fighting for breath. " I only borrowed it. If Ballantyne hadn't smashed the window I shouldn't have thought of it. It was the landlord's fault, not mine. The money was for him. He said he'd report me if I didn't give it to him. I didn't have it. He took it. He was to blame."

Kenton's voice became a whine, and trailed off into convulsive sobs. For a moment longer the Head stood looking at Kenton. Then he moved aside from the doorway and spoke.

" You can go to your dormitory, Kenton," he said. " To-morrow you will be expelled. I shall see the landlord of the ' Peal o' Bells ' about the part he has played in this affair. That is all. Go."

Kenton dragged himself across the room and out into the passage. His shuffling footfall died away in the distance.

The Head turned to the others a face whose expression, although stern, was suddenly of a different kind.

" I am very pleased with you four boys," he said. " I wish to thank you for so effectively clearing up this odious affair."

Solemnly he shook hands with each one, and a twinkle came into his eye.

" Perhaps it would not be politic to inquire how you got out of your house to-night," he went on, " but I think it would be better for you to return in a more orthodox manner. Here is a key to the front door of your house. At present the best thing for us all is to go to bed. To-morrow morning, in assembly, I shall tell the school what has happened to-night. Once again, thank you all very much for what you have done. Good-night."

"Well, that's that," said Darrell, when they were in the quadrangle. "Phew! I'm jolly glad it's over. We ought to celebrate to-morrow."

"You bet," said Collinson. "It's turned out a jolly sight better than it did last time we broke out."

Suddenly Darrell stopped.

"I say," he said. "Do you realize that we are in the quadrangle when every one else is in bed? We have a key to the front door of the house. In my study are those old clothes, still tied up in a convenient bundle. Over there is Cody's statue."

"You mean?" whispered Larkin.

"I do," said Darrell.

Next morning, when the school streamed out of assembly, a great crowd gathered round Darrell to offer him their apologies.

"Sorry, Darrell," they said. "Dashed sorry and all that. Might have known it was blinking rot."

"Oh, that's all right," growled Darrell,

brusque in his embarrassment. " Oh, shut up, it's all right."

" But it isn't all right," said one and another. " We were a lot of rotters ever to have thought you took that money."

" For heaven's sake, shut up," said Darrell. " Run away and leave me in peace."

" Dashed sorry, Darrell," went on the crowd. " Honestly——"

And then, to Darrell's relief, there came a sudden diversion.

Raymond was running across the quadrangle, waving his arms and shouting at the top of his voice.

" Come on, you chaps ! " he yelled. " Come and look at Cody's statue ! "

The crowd flowed across the quadrangle, cheering ; massing at the edge of Mr. Cody's garden, it stood, roaring with laughter.

Mr. Cody's statue had been carefully decorated. On the head, at a rakish angle, was fixed a battered bowler hat. Drawn tight round the trunk was a faded old frock-coat, slit here and there to accommodate the ample proportions of the figure. The face had been rendered more startling than ever by means of green and yellow crayons. The statue now bore a woeful resemblance to an elderly and bibulous gentleman after a night out.

Practically the whole school had gathered by the time Mr. Cody came out. At sight of Julius Cæsar's regalia, Mr. Cody stood still, his face turning a shade of purple.

" Who," he shouted, " has done this ? "

But the crowd paid no need to him, and Mr. Cody turned on his heel and made for the Head's house. And in a few minutes he returned with the Head following at a more sedate pace.

" This—this incredible desecration," panted Mr. Cody, " has been perpetrated on my statue. I demand that the culprit be found. I—I——" He stopped for want of breath.

The Head stared, coughed, and smiled.

" I shall . . ." he said, with an effort. " I shall . . ."

But that was as far as he got. The thing was too much for him, and in front of the furious Mr. Cody, Dr. Alcott burst out laughing.

Then he turned and walked rapidly away, with his handkerchief pressed to his lips, leaving Mr. Cody trembling with rage. And to crown Mr. Cody's mortification, the Head admonished the offenders publicly at breakfast on the following day, but did nothing to establish their identity, and let the matter drop.

A few days later Darrell took his reconstituted First Eleven to an away match against St. Peter's College, a school that Melhurst had never previously played. The home team was beaten by a hundred and one runs, Darrell hitting up a hundred and six in a little over two hours. By the time stumps were drawn the St. Peter's crowd was reduced to the wildest rumours concerning the Melhurst captain.

" Obviously a county man," they declared. " Probably an old boy whom they've brought along with them. A fellow who can hit our fast bowlers all over the place like that can only be a county man."

And when they reached the Melhurst gates on their return journey the First Eleven found a large crowd waiting to greet them. The match with St. Peter's was the last game of a highly successful season. Melhurst had played fifteen games, won ten, and drawn three.

When the news of Darrell's performance was known a great shout went up.

"Darrell!" shouted the crowd. "Hooray for Darrell!"

So great was the noise that it drew the Head to his study window. He stood gazing down with a thoughtful look on his face.

"Indeed!" said the Head. "*Indeed!*"

Chapter XVIII

AU REVOIR, MELHURST!

THE Rev. Pelham Alcott, headmaster of Melhurst, leaned forward in his study chair and pressed the bell on the desk before him.

"Have Mr. Darrell of Reed's House sent to me, will you, Baxter," he said to his butler a few moments later. "I don't think he has gone yet."

The butler bowed and withdrew.

As the door closed the Head rose and approached the open window. As he gazed down at the quadrangle he frowned and tapped the window-sill with his fingers.

Below him was a scene of confusion. All over the quadrangle were boxes and portmanteaux, for this was the last day of the summer term. Some boys were standing about, exchanging gossip of holiday plans, others were hurrying to and fro, whilst others again were emerging from the buildings. Amid the throng the porters laboured, carrying luggage to waiting cars and station coaches.

But the Head saw little of this ; he turned away and began pacing up and down the room, as though preoccupied with a problem. Then he came back to the window, his fingers tapping restlessly as before.

Suddenly there was a tap at the door, and in response to his " Come in," a tall dark boy of about eighteen entered the room.

" Ah, here you are, Darrell," said the Head genially. " Sit down, will you ? " He motioned him to a chair. " Had a good term ? "

" Yes, thank you, sir."

The Head sat down in his own chair on the other side of the desk and gazed intently at the new-comer.

" I have sent for you, Darrell," he said, in a different tone, " because I have something important to say to you. It is this. Goulding has decided not to come back next term. He is going up to Oxford sooner than he expected. For the past few days I have been considering whom to appoint as his successor as captain of the school. And I have decided to offer the school captaincy to you."

" Me, sir ? " gasped the astonished Darrell.

" Yes. You are better at games than Goulding was, and your work this term has been quite good. From Mr. Cody's account you don't seem to have particularly distinguished yourself at mathematics, but there is nothing to complain of as regards any other subject. This, Darrell, is a great improvement on your past record. As a prefect you have steadied down and overcome difficulties of more than one kind. And your leadership at cricket seems to be popular with the other boys."

Darrell had been listening with an indefinable expression on his face. At this point he leaned forward and asked :

" Sir, are you offering me the captaincy, or telling me I must take it ? "

The Head picked up a pencil and tapped on the desk before him.

" You know, Darrell," he said, " I suspected that this might happen again."

" You're not going to make me school captain, are you, sir, as you made me a prefect, even though I don't want to be captain ? " he pleaded.

The Head considered this remark for a minute.

" I tell you what I will do, Darrell," he said at length. " I will leave the matter over till next term. And in any case, if I offer the captaincy to Humphreys, say, he has only another term at school, so that there will be plenty of time to bring up the question again."

" You mean, sir, that eventually there will be no . . . escape for me ? "

" Who knows ? " answered the Head. " Who knows ? You are a strange boy, Darrell."

" Anyhow, thank you, sir," said Darrell, relieved at his respite.

Believing the interview to be at an end, he got up to go. Just as he reached the door, however, the Head's voice stopped him.

" By the way, Darrell, I wanted to ask you something else."

He turned and moved back again.

" How was it that Kenton owed so *much* money to the landlord of the ' Peal o' Bells ' ? "

" Oh, making whoopee, sir."

" Making whoopee ? "

" Yes, sir. Going on the snurge. I mean, sir, having a good time."

" Ah, thank you," murmured the Head.

" Good-bye, sir," said Darrell. " I hope you have good holidays."

" Thank you, Darrell, thank you. And be sure to have a good time yourself."

" You bet I will," said Darrell to himself when the door had closed between them.

Inside the study the Head approached the window again. The crowd in the quadrangle was thinning. Soon all the boys would have gone, and he himself could forget them for a while.

The Head was spending the major part of his holidays at Deauville, and as he thought of Deauville his eyes gleamed. The career of a schoolmaster was all very well, of course, but there were times when even the most equable of schoolmasters had had enough of boys for a while—of boys, and staff, and school routine with its almost endless variety of problems.

Deauville beckoned a tired schoolmaster—Deauville, blue skies and glittering seas, palms, and the casino. . . .

" Whoopee ! " murmured the Head to himself, and cut a solemn caper on his carpet.

Down below, from the basement of his house, he could hear voices and laughter. The army of cleaners invaded the school with pails and scrubbing-brushes.

Presently the largest school gates clanged behind the last departing boy. Desolation settled on the great group of buildings.

Melhurst was shut for the summer holidays.

THE END

PRINTED IN GREAT BRITAIN AT
THE PRESS OF THE PUBLISHERS